Man o' the World

# Man o' the World
by
Graham Ashworth

**ISBN:** 978-0-9574346-3-9

Man o' the World

**Man o' the World**
**by**
**Graham Ashworth**

**ISBN:** 978-0-9574346-3-9



Disclaimer: All characters appearing in this work are fictitious. Any resemblance to real persons, living or dead is purely coincidental.

Published by

i2i
PUBLISHING

i2i Publishing. Manchester.
**www.i2ipublishing.co.uk**

## Preface

*Take those twenty six letters of the alphabet that you first saw colourfully painted on the wall as a small child. Put them into words, so that as you grew, more were learned each day. Then neatly arrange them into an order that could hopefully spark the imagination of someone, who might just one day consider reading them.*

*Graham Ashworth*

**Dedication**
I would like to thank Nick for her invaluable technical contribution. Also thanks to my publisher Lionel Ross of i2i Publishing for advice and support.
But my special thanks go to Dawn for believing when belief was needed!

*Graham Ashworth*

**Prologue**

Discarding his work clothes into an unruly pile, the young man never gave the slightest thought to the sorcery behind their removal, cleansing, ironing and replacement in his robust Edwardian chest of drawers.

Dancing as he dressed, not to any particularly co-ordinated movements; it was just getting ready to go out bopping. A one finger salute to the poster of Billy was done with recognition of his new found idol's influence. Swiftly pulling on his white y-fronts, he fondly and wholeheartedly gave his package a squeeze, in order to signify the knowledge of its forthcoming venture.

Donning his second-best clothes was done with a smoothness that mirrored his confidence. His new *'John Collier, John Collier the window to watch'* suit would have to wait for a more suitable occasion. Heading to the bathroom, he reached past his father's shaving foam and brush, then beyond the rusting tin of Brylcream to sample the aftershave that lurked beyond. But taking one sniff had the effect of crumpling his face in disgust, before returning the offending item with no regard to its original location. The fresh smell of soap and water would have to suffice, it seemed.
'Bloody hell, it's all new to me and boy oh boy, it sounds fantastic.' But there was no time now for self-administered relief. So it's on with the winkle pickers, then off into the unknown to discover more of the

delights that surrounded his new-found sexual enlightenment.

**Chapter 1**

"Time to go Ray!"
The tired landlord nudged the bleary-eyed, yellow skinned man in the ill-fitting suit.

"You'd nodded off."

"Must be the company!" He found it within himself to joke. Then taking the effort to survey the room he added, "Quiet, isn't it?"

"Yeh, not really worth opening on Mondays and Tuesdays anymore," he wearily replied.

Ray could remember when he would revel in the company of others any day of the week. But the ageing town centre pubs, once his playground, were shutting down at an alarming rate. Once, he would feel it his duty, over the seven days of the week, to be seen in as many as possible and in turn he would be fondly known in whichever he chose to frequent.

Constantly he would recall the smoky, stale alcohol stench of the now torn-down, slum-like hostelries. In their heyday, even these hovels would be run by licensees with an iron fist. They would make their entrance at around 10pm on a weekend evening to greet their appreciative public. Landladies in particular were a hard, no-nonsense type and woe-betide anyone who crossed them. 'Done up to the nines,' with a heavy layer of make-up and a bouffant hairstyle, the landlady would take her seat at the bar, not unlike royalty. Her cronies would then gather around with flattery in abundance, in order to hopefully be invited for A.T.'s, (after time drinking.)

The riff raff and other undesirables would be singled out to leave at closing time, leaving the clique to carry on drinking behind closed doors.

But home for Ray is a cold, lonely, empty place these days. The lifestyle he chose, as a 'man o' the world' would see to that. The entertainer, joker, story-teller's audiences had all but gone.

## Chapter 2 June 1961

Pausing at the hallway mirror, Ray liked what he saw. His efforts to simulate the look of his idol, Billy Fury, were beginning to have a large impact on his life. Closing the door behind him, leather jacket over his shoulder, a confident swagger led him down the red brick council estate avenue. Humming and whistling, combined with a poor vocal rendition of 'Halfway to Paradise,' did nothing to detract from his new image.

The re-creation had also not gone unnoticed at his destination; a fifteen minute walk to the large detached houses across town which would see him at a place he could once, only have dreamed of.

Lorraine Faraday couldn't actually believe what was going on. The scruffy, uncouth kid who had left the no-hopers school only twelve months ago had taken her breath away. And that was not all; her dream of moving into womanhood with fairytale romance, had been uncontrollably scuppered. It should have been one of the Elliott twins; tall, blond and the object of desire of almost every girl at St Catherine's Grammar School. All through her three years of flirting and occasional dating with one or the other, she had managed to save herself for the right moment. But that didn't arise as planned. Just one date with Ray 'bloody' Taylor and wham bam, gone! But still, she herself had discovered this re-designed, if a little rugged, diamond of a young man and would refine him accordingly.

# Man o' the World

Something had been on Ray's mind all morning and his plans were to push the boundaries into the unknown. Overhearing a conversation on the building site where he had laboured for the last six months had excited him beyond belief.

"What she can't do with her cherry red lips and tantalising tongue isn't worth knowing."

And with the images portrayed inside his head drawn from the graphic details, he knew where his fantasises could be realised. That toffee-nosed Lorraine Faraday would oblige before being kicked into touch.

Everything was going to plan; he could have achieved his aim and still be in the pub for 4.00pm. The fact that he was underage did nothing to deter him from his new found thirst for pub life. Fridays saw the site closed for the weekends at lunchtime, usually with a one way procession to the nearest boozer. Ray was the only one who deviated from the early session start, the mid morning eavesdropping saw to that.

The last part of his intended route took him through Brook Wood. But freezing at the sound of splitting timber followed by a capitulating crash, unnerved his macho spirit. Considering a run for it, he asserted himself to investigate.

"Fucking hell, you nearly made me shit myself!" And surveying the unique sight before him, he added, "what are you doing, you daft twat?"

At first, nothing in the way of an explanation left the huge man's lips, but eventually he muttered "Can't even top myself properly."

"Blocky you pillock, what would you want to top yourself for?"

"It's nowt."

"Nowt? You're sat with a rope round your neck and a tree branch round your head and you say nowt!"

"It's Shirley, she's chucked me."

"Is that all? I thought something was really up."

"Is that all! Piss off while I find a stronger tree."

"Come on Blocky, nobody's worth that. Anyway it's not meant to be. Look, in theory it should have been strong enough. That branch is ten inches thick. Somebody somewhere is saying it's not your time yet, if you believe that sort of shit."

"I suppose so" almost mutely left his lips.

"Come on, we're going to the pub."

"I can't I'm skint," he meekly answered.

"Bloody hell, you know how to push it don't you."

"Haven't you got anyone else to go with? We don't usually hang out."

"Well we do now. And anyway, where I was going first can wait, let's get tanked up. Come on, we're wasting valuable supping time."

## Chapter 3

"Ah, Ray boy, will you be joining us?" Jimmy looked up from his hand of cards with a smile that showed no warmth.

"Too right, here's ten bob Blocky, go 'n' get a couple of pints," and handed over a crisp ten shilling note. The buzz of the tap room had already hooked him. Here, jokes would be swapped, sport argued upon and the world's problems philosophised.

"Money to burn eh Ray?"

"Money to fleece you lot with." His cocky confident retort delivered with immaculate rebuff.

Jimmy Knight had the reputation of a hard case and a fiery temper; the type of man you would choose to be on your side in a fight.

"Let's see the colour of your money then Ray boy." So, in doing so, he reached into his back pocket and slapped his entire wage packet onto the shiny polished table. The four other players looked gleefully at the small square brown envelope.

"He means business, Jimmy," Haggis stated, with mocked seriousness, in a sharp Glaswegian accent.

"We better beware then boys or our kids will be going hungry tonight." Jimmy straightened his slouched back as he spoke with insincere joviality.

Ray was beginning to get a little anxious. Half-an-hour into the game and he was losing money, hand over fist. It's only three card brag he told himself, luck would surely even itself out eventually. Then sensing an end to the ill-gotten gains, Jimmy coldly asked,

"Yer not thinking of wimping out are you Ray?"

"No, it's just that I'll have to keep some board money back."

"Ah yes, money for Mammy; don't worry if you lose it, I could lend you some 'til next Friday." Loan sharking could be a profitable business amongst these losers.

Looking into the eyes of the other players, Jimmy's and Haggis' were as cold as ice. Reg's were quite neutral, but Arnie's, a usually quiet spoken sort, were shouting out 'go while you can.'

"Ok, a couple more hands," he relented.

"That's the boy." Jimmy's encouragement to be one of the gang made him feel good.

Down to his last five shillings, Ray was now of the opinion 'ah well, its shit or bust.' Then becoming aware of a subtle movement across the other side of the tap room, he noticed Blocky straining his neck in short jerking movements. Looking over with a puzzled crease in his brow, he saw he was beckoning him over.

"Just going for a piss," Ray announced.

"Yeh, you go 'n' point Percy at the porcelain and your luck will change when you get back," Haggis laughed at his own unoriginality.

Following Ray into the gents, Blocky whispered through a tight jaw, "he's cheating."

"What?" Ray blurted.

"His deck is marked."

"How do you know?"

"Because he uses the same method as me."

"Go on," Ray encouraged.

"You see the intricate blue pattern on the back of the cards, well there are tiny marks hidden amongst the squiggles, you wouldn't see them unless you knew."

"Are you sure?" Ray looked for absolute confirmation. But before an answer was forthcoming, the door swung open.

"So this is where all the dicks hang out!" Jimmy's humourless tone echoed around the basic facilities, as he unzipped his flies beside the two youths. "You two have been a while; you're not thinking of leaving are you?"

"No, we're on our way back now."

"Good lads, that's good."

At the restart, Ray could see it immediately. Not sure what each mark meant, the fact that they were there was enough.

"Are these your own cards Jimmy?" Ray almost shocked himself by his own outburst.

"What the fuck has that got to do with anything?"

"They are marked." A false confident calmness left his lips.

"Are you calling me a fucking cheat?" Jimmy was in no mood for cocky teenagers. Haggis and the others were quick to get out of the way, knowing what was coming next.

Rising to his feet, fist already clenched, the table toppled over as he lunged for Ray. No lightweight himself he was high in the pecking order of school scrappers, but he was in no way, any sort of match for

Jimmy. A burst of heavy punches rained down on Ray's face, giving rise to painful flashes at each blow.

Sensing the cease of the onslaught, Ray uncurled himself from his foetal position on the floor, just in time to witness Blocky with his hands around the bully's neck. Some of the others were trying to remove his grip without success.

"Blocky stop, you'll kill him!" Ray found himself upside the pair. But he was so fixated in his task, no words from the outside world penetrated into his brain. "Blocky that's enough!" Ray shouted and finally he slowly started to remove his grip. "That's it Blocky, leave him now," Ray's voice, calming his friend down, bringing him back to comprehension.

The whole pub was stunned into silence, only the landlord moved to check the condition of the casualty slumped in the corner. "He'll live," he sighed with relief. The last thing he wanted was the police turning up, putting his licence at risk. Then asserting himself, his finger singled out the two upstarts,

"You two out, you're barred."

"Not without my money, that bastard was cheating."

"Ok, get your own money and not a penny more."

So picking up his weeks wages, a sore Ray and his silent partner left.

"Fucking hell Blocky; where did that come from?" Ray eventually asked as they took a seat on the park bench.

"Where did what come from?"

"You, taking Jimmy out like that. I've not seen you have an argument, never mind a fight."

"Never needed to." His uncomplicated reply hung in the air.

"Well I'm glad I never crossed you; you could have killed him, do you know that?"

"Never thought about it."

"Well it's a good job you didn't, or you could have swung for it."

Then the irony of the unwitting statement hit home, leaving the two comrades in fits of laughter.

**Chapter 4** **September 1963**

"Something for the weekend Ray?"

George, his barber quietly enquired out of the corner of his mouth, almost as if the mere mention could be considered blasphemous.

"What? Oh Yeh, I suppose I better had." He knew their use would only be a passing phase, like eating a sweet with the wrapper still on, he reflected. But his recent journey to the pox clinic had unnerved him somewhat. The stories he had heard before his attendance, of umbrella scrapes down his japs eye, had proved unfounded. A course of penicillin and a lot of awkward questions were enough to deter another visit though. Anyway, he knew the culprit, it was that slapper he picked up on the Blackpool charabanc outing.

Earlier, as he sat waiting for his turn in the swivel chair he had considered a Beatle cut, but settled on his usual flick back, tried and tested style. Anyway, he would sure look a right pillock when this Liverpool lot's popularity fizzled out over the next few months, as surely it would. Yeh, keep the hair the same, the girls love it, when they flicked their manicured fingers through his quiff, they were putty in his hands. That and plain fucking stupid; tell them what they want to hear and bingo, another notch.

Lorraine Faraday however, did manage to see through him after a couple of dates; his unreliability and impatience were the main factors for their split, not to mention his outrageous demands. Well, he sure didn't want to piss about holding hands and walks in the park. 'Let's take things slowly' she'd said in that girly-girly way; *bollocks to that!* Ray sniffed at the memory. Blocky too had more or less taken a different path. He still considered him a mate, but at times he could be hard work. One way conversations were not unusual, whilst he himself was fluent in bullshit. Let's hope it works on his date for tonight; now she *is* a looker, could even be said to be out of his league. But that is never going to stop Ray Taylor.

Picking up his jacket from the coat stand by the exit, the devil inside got the better of him.

"Heh George, when you gonna get shut of that stupid 'Irish jig' on your head?"

"You cheeky bugger, this is only temporary; a cure for baldness is just around the corner, mark my words."

Then before closing the door behind him, Ray shouted with a twinkle in his eye,

"In your dreams George, in your dreams."

## Chapter 5

"The Great Escape; not what I would have chosen, but I suppose it will have to do," Val shrugged.

*Me neither, straight down to the nitty-gritty would be preferable;* Ray's thought process was as predictable as ever. But in all honesty he knew this was going to be no ordinary date. Valerie Sanderson is, to put it in one word, stunning. So a couple of hours inside the Odeon cinema would give him time to gather his wits and plan his strategy.

Stopping at the much besought back row, Val continued past him down the steps to a more central seating area. *Oh well. Just go along with it all,* Ray sighed.

Casting a sideways glance part-way through the trailers, he considered his first move. *'Give her a peck on the cheek to sweeten her up a little, then slide yer hand over to her bra'*. But the more he thought about it, the more this move seemed stupid. *'Ok then'*, he pondered, *'arm around the shoulder first'*. *'No, not that either'*, as Val caught his eye with a warm smile. So settling upon delaying tactics, he just placed his hand beside his own thigh. A few moments later Val's hand was a fraction away from his left little finger. Closing his eyes he imagined the two digits touching. As the reality finally happened after numerous tiny movements, it felt like electricity was flowing between them.

The film had already started but he couldn't recall one thing that had happened on screen. *'What's up with you, you great soft prick?'* he asked of himself. The only physical contact throughout the whole cinematic experience was the linking of their smallest fingers. But to Ray it outshone any of his numerous sexual encounters.

Nerves were beginning to get the better of him as they opened the door to the San Remo Cafe; he was none too sure of what was going on. Two large coffees were placed before them by a tired-looking, overweight, middle-aged, you would assume, Italian woman.

"Thank you," Val's voice to Ray was like velvet.

"So Ray, tell me about yourself."

"Nowt to tell really." Shit, he was sounding like Blocky. "I mean I'm just an ordinary guy, ordinary home, ordinary job."

"What is your job?" Val tried to encourage the conversation to flow.

"I'm working at the pressings factory." Ray wasn't really in the mood to talk of his latest dead end job.

"What does that involve?"

"Not a lot really, the machine does all the work. I just keep a check on the parts that pop out, make sure they are all the same." As he reeled off his job description he was embarrassed by his lack of ambition. So quickly turning the question around, he enquired of her employment status.

"I'm a secretary in a solicitors but I intend to study law and move up within the company," Val proudly boasted.

"Wow, you must be really bright."

"No Ray, I'm like you, just an ordinary person, but I've got determination to succeed."

"You're no ordinary woman." Ray's voice tailed off as he realised flattery was not appropriate within this conversation.

"Listen Ray, let's think of a vocation that would really suit you," and weighing him up with a cute curling of her lips, she offered, "Police, what about a career in the police?"

Ray spluttered and nearly choked on his coffee.

"The police?" he repeated with incredulity.

"Yeh, you haven't got a police record have you?"

"No no, just a few minor skirmishes when I was younger; a clip around the earhole, that sort of thing."

"Well then, you should be ok."

"Nah, I don't think so, not for me." Ray completely blocked the notion from his head.

"The GPO then, working as a telephone engineer?" Val searched for something more suitable.

"Hmmm, sounds ok." The word 'engineer' was a worry. It sounded too technical but he would not reveal that to Val just yet.

"Come on Ray, you must have thought about your ideal job?"

"Don't laugh but I always wanted to be a pilot; you know, passenger airlines, around the world, exotic locations and all that," his childhood dream resurfaced.

"Well I'm not going to knock your dreams but maybe we should stay a little closer to the ground." There was a sparkle in her eye that diffused any hint that it was in any way patronising.

"Ok then, we'll give Mr Boeing a wide berth for now." Ray tried to reciprocate with a glint in his own green eyes.

Then leaning forward, she carefully bit her bottom lip as she touched both his shoulders, in a way as if to weigh up his frame,

"I've got it, a fireman. You'd make a perfect fireman. What do you say?"

"Never thought about it, do you think so?"

"Yeh I do. I tell you what; I'll find out how you go about applying and get back to you, how does that sound?"

"Yeh sounds great."

"Come on then, I think they're waiting to lock up."

Walking Val home felt like someone had put foam rubber in the soles of his shoes and only in the last two hundred yards did he dare slide his hand into hers. Reaching the end of the garden path at her parent's semi, she released her hand and without a pause, pecked Ray on the cheek. Then turning at the door with a final smile, she was gone. Touching the exact point of contact on his face, he reflected, their walk had been conducted in virtual silence. No mention of another date, or his possible venture into a new career. It was almost as if further discussion would ruin what for Ray, was a perfect evening. He had even resisted the urge to say that he was more of a 'hands on' type of guy, during the earlier conversation. At that point he could have placed his hands near her breasts, along with his cheeky grin. That sort of thing usually worked and would lead to other things. But what was happening to him? What was it with Valerie Sanderson?

**Chapter 6** **November 1963**

"What would you want to leave a good sound job like this for?" Ray actually believed Harry, his foreman at the pressings factory, considered this to be good employment.

"I've made my mind up Harry. I've applied and been accepted by the fire brigade."

"Are you sure you're cut out for that kind of work?" Harry quizzed him.

"How hard can it be? Anyone can squirt water and hold a blanket out to catch someone jumping from a burning building."

"You haven't really thought this through have you Ray? I think you have watched too many Tommy Trinder films." Harry was aghast at Ray's impetuous behaviour.

"I'm handing in my notice, I start next Monday. Me, and three other lads from town are to be at the fire brigade training centre, first thing Monday."

"Well I think you are being a bit foolish, but it's up to you." Harry turned away, shaking his head in disbelief.

At least Ray's mother was happy,

"I'm glad you're starting to grow up, our Ray. This and that lovely girl you're courting, she's calmed you down."

It was true, he had changed beyond recognition. The pubs and the snooker hall would soon be sending out search parties for him, he imagined.

As for Val, she hadn't intended to mould and control Ray; it's just that he was so compliant to her wishes. His reputation as 'Jack the lad' so far appeared unfounded. But she was no fool, leopards changing spots and all those other clichés would have to remain at the forefront of her mind.

So for now she would see him off to twelve weeks of intense training. She hadn't mentioned how physical and military based his course would be, better let him find out first hand and then see if her young boyfriend would come back a man.

## Chapter 7

Ray was exhausted, both mentally and physically. It was only three days into his training and he was ready to quit. Attempting to shine his shoes up as the others had done was proving difficult if not impossible. One of the instructors, John Conrad, had it in for him it seemed. Screaming and bawling into his face at a distance of six inches away, made him shudder. Halitosis and spittle were still firmly etched in the pores of his skin.

"What the fuck am I doing here?" He eventually yelled out, and throwing his shoes to the ground he continued, "I don't need this shit, I'm off."

"Whoa, Ray," Barry, one of the other lads grabbed his arm.

"If I wanted to be treated like this, I would have become a squaddie!" He attempted to remove the grip as he finally flipped.

"No Ray, calm down, it's all a game." Barry tried to reassure him.

"What? It's pure bastardisation; that's not a game in my book."

"You just have to play along, let them think they have broken you, and then it will all become easier when they have you toeing the line."

"Do you think so?" Ray wasn't so sure.

"I know so. Listen, our kid is already in the job. He says it's only usually for the first week or so then they have to knuckle down and train us properly."

"Is he already on station?"

"Yeh, he loves it. I went there to learn a bit more in advance, you know, see how it all works."

"And?" Ray questioned.

"And it's the bee's knees."

"In what way?" Ray was all ears.

"Well, day-shifts are quite structured, drills, cleaning, lectures, that sort of thing." Barry paused for effect. "But nights, that's another kettle of fish. After a few checks and odd jobs, the time's your own."

"What do you mean?" Ray wasn't sure where this was leading.

"You haven't really looked into this have you Ray?"

"Not really, no," he admitted.

"Well, after supper, that's the evening meal, not anywhere near what you would call suppertime, usually about 8.30pm, then its recreation time." Barry's eyes glinted at the prospect.

"Recreation time?" Ray felt a little stupid repeating Barry's words, but he just didn't know.

"You can play snooker, darts, cards, or just watch telly if you're so inclined."

"Are you joking?" Ray was no gullible fool.

"No kidding. There's a bar to help you unwind."

"Piss off!" Now he knew he was being mocked.

"Of course the gaffers expect you to study for promotion exams at some point during this time, but show a little willing and they're happy."

Still not quite sure if he was being ridiculed, Ray searched Barry's eyes for clues and reading Ray's thoughts, he reaffirmed his words,

"It's all true. And then when the white dot has gone from the telly and you've played your last hand of cards, its bed time." Barry held out his hands in order to signify, 'how good does it get?'

"Now you are taking the piss."

"No, ask anyone, it's a perk to make up for the poor wages and long shifts; they have to let you sleep by law."

"Yeh, I know the pay isn't brilliant is it?" Ray had at least taken the trouble to find out about the wages.

"No, but you can do another job on your days off, cash in hand. What else can you do?"

"I worked on the building sites."

"Can you bricky?" Barry enquired.

"Yeh, I can to a reasonable standard."

"There you are then, do some bricklaying on your days off."

"I'm not going freezing my tits off in the middle of winter again!" Ray exclaimed.

"You don't have to. You just work when it suits you. Do jobs for family and friends, more will come from word of mouth; it's only extra cash after all."

"Bloody hell, you make it sound like being down the working men's club."

"Exactly, just like the club, only you're getting paid at the same time." Barry felt like he had finally gotten through.

"So Ray, are you sticking with it or not?" Barry's face was beaming at him.

"Well, if you put it like that," Ray smirked. "Anyhow, I've got this stupid short back-and-sides haircut now."

"That's it Ray, now let's have a look at those shoes, see if we can't get 'em looking like shaving mirrors."

## Chapter 8

So Ray completed his training three months later; not exactly with flying colours! Some of the instructors were not entirely convinced of his commitment to the fire service as a career. But one thing they all agreed upon; he was definitely a character and that was the one thing that was needed in today's modern 1960's brigade.

John Conrad eventually conceded defeat in trying to break Ray after around ten weeks of vicious bullying. He also lost his two shilling bet that he could make him quit.

It was during his time at the training centre that Ray took up his old school habit of smoking. At various times through the physical aspects of his course, a 'smokeo' break would be called and all smokers and non-smokers alike would huddle into a small hidey-hole room for their fix. Feeling slightly cheated if he didn't partake, his lifelong addiction to tobacco had well and truly re-emerged.

Stories would also be swapped in efforts to prolong the length of the respite. This is where he would come into his own. Old stories and jokes would be reinvented and made his own. At times, someone's story would return to them via Ray who was convinced it was unique to him, himself. One story in particular would be used throughout his whole career.

A practice still used to this day is to 'get a stand in,' someone to take your shift. Allegedly once, at a change of watch, one particular fireman was missing and in his place a plumber, overalls and all, stood waiting the commencement of the shift. When questioned on his return to duty about his absence he stated that he was told if he needed time off, he could get a mate to stand in for him. Obviously the procedure meant a colleague of the same qualifications, but his interpretation was somewhat confused. So in developing this story, Ray was actually in attendance at the event and even attributed its infamy to one particular unfortunate fireman, sacked early in his career.

So at its conclusion, twenty two of the twenty eight course starters were posted to various fire stations throughout the area. Ray Taylor, Barry Carter, Len Holloway and John Rudge squeezed into an ageing Ford Anglia, along with their laden kit-bags, to go and help make their town a safer place.

## Chapter 9

"Heh Ray, will you be at the church service next Sunday?"

Piss off!" Ray was still seething, especially at Barry, who was in on the joke due to his prior knowledge of life on station.

Father Martin, the brigade chaplain had delivered an excellent sermon. Actually just another fireman from a different shift, Marty Gorman had posed as protector of the men's souls. Brilliantly portrayed to new, 'red-arse' recruits, the fictitious ceremony was getting more believable each time it was played out. Hymns were sung, psalms read, culminating in wine and unleavened bread after the fireman's prayer. Not done in view of any fire brigade hierarchy; Sunday evenings were the perfect time, as all officers had long since left for home.

"Don't fret Ray, you'll be in on it next time." Barry was still chuckling at the thought of Ray singeing his hair as he leant over the alter candle. Ray wouldn't mind but he had been on the lookout for 'wind ups' since his first day, but this was so utterly believable.

Sensing a change of subject was overdue, Barry paused for a short while before moving into totally new territory.

"Do you know that everything we do in this life is pre-determined?"

"Fuck off, you're getting all deep and preachy again." Ray was almost ready to turn in for the night. Everyone else had left to get their heads down;

leaving the two excitable newcomers to wait in anticipation of what seemed the elusive next fire call.

"No Ray, I've read this book about something called the 'big bang.' Albert Einstein and a bloke by the name of Hubble are mentioned in it."

"Big bang? I've had a few of them in my time." Ray lowered the tone by his contribution.

"I'll try 'n' explain; about 13 billion years ago, the universe burst into life with a big bang." Ray put his hand to his mouth to fake a yawn. Undeterred, Barry continued. "Now we, all the people on earth are living for a short space of time, relatively speaking that is. Then everything will die; all the planets, stars, everything, over the next few billion years."

"And?" Ray looked thoroughly bored as his friend philosophically reeled off his spiel.

"And, in my opinion everything will contract then, explode and start again."

"Is that it?" Ray scoffed.

"No Ray, the point is, if it all starts again and we are born again, everything we do must happen again, it's got to, exactly the same as before."

"Well I won't get caught out with that bloody church service, that's for sure."

"Oh yes you will. You can't change anything."

"Why not?" Ray was lost.

"Well all your ancestors could have done things differently; met someone else, died in an accident, or anything, right up to your Mum and Dad making you. So if you are born again, what would make you so special to be able to change things?"

"I just would do things differently," Ray shrugged.

"Ah, you're missing the point." Barry gave up.

*"No, the point is, I'm missing my bed." Ray* found the opportunity to get to his feet. But just as he took to the stairs from the mess area, a loud thud sprung the fire station into life. Lights in every corner of the building illuminated, quickly followed by an ear piercing two tone alarm.

Ray found he was trembling at the prospect of his first fire. Taking up position in the crew cab, he was dressed and ready for action before the engine had moved from the station forecourt.

"Persons reported," was the cry from the front cab. This was the most serious scenario for the firemen, as someone was reported to be trapped inside the burning building. His heart felt as though it would burst as adrenaline pumped around his veins with increased pressure.

Expectations of brightly coloured flames were quickly replaced with the reality of a blanket of suffocating black smoke pouring out of the property into the street. His first task took him away and into fresh air to find a fire hydrant, in order to replenish the water tank contained within the appliance.

Unbelievably, within minutes everything was scaled down to a sedate, even pace. Windows not already shattered were opened to allow smoke to ventilate from the terraced house. At this point Ray and Barry were beckoned into the hallway by George Kendal, their officer in charge.

"Right you two, before we go inside, take in this smell."

Ray and Barry looked at each other, as if for clues. "This smell, you won't get to experience it too often thankfully, but you'll never forget it, believe me."

The sickly stench emitting from the living room was that of burning flesh. In no way the same as cooking meat, it had a synthetic additive, probably caused by the casualties' clothing. Tears were running down Ray's face, not in any way due to the old man's demise or the sight of a partially burned corpse. The acrid gases of burning materials stung his eyes like acid.

The aftermath of the fire, initially a strange experience would become a familiar ritual over the coming years. Noses and mouths blackened with toxic smoke would be confounded by the addition of cigarette smoke, as the men lit up at the first opportunity. Banter would then kick in, that to an outsider would appear disrespectful to say the least. It's just the way it is, in order to cope with the experiences that sometimes no one should ever have the misfortune to witness.

In a way, Ray had found his true vocation. His ability to laugh and joke, but moreover selectively black out inconvenient aspects of life, would suit him right down to the ground, both at work and in his outside life.

## Chapter 10 May 1965

Val gave up, even with two pennies on the arm of the record player. The new Hollies single was still slipping. A little like life itself she reflected, alarm bells have began to ring in her life, as well as those of a different kind in Rays. Switching on the transistor radio for company, she found she couldn't tune in to any decent music, so settled for silence instead.

A tap at the door was followed by Ray's pinafore attired mother peering around the newly created opening.

"Is it alright to come in?"

"Yes, of course Mrs Taylor." Val meekly smiled at the sight of her pinny-clad would-be mother in law. The number of times she had insisted upon 'Edith' or 'Edie', but it had fallen on deaf ears as far as Val was concerned. She was brought up with strong values and always addressing older generations with Mr or Mrs was one of them.

"Cup o' tea for you, lovey?"

"Oh thanks, I'm ready for one right now."

"You shouldn't be doing that in your condition, put them brushes away and wait for our Raymond to do it."

But the look returned by Val said it all.

'And how long would we be waiting?' And an understanding nod in acknowledgement spoke volumes about the organised chaos that surrounded her son's life.

"I'm so sorry about last night. I don't even know why he turned up." Ray's father had decided to pay a visit to the family home after a two year absence.

"It's ok Mrs Taylor; it's not your fault."

Absolutely steaming drunk, he parked his backside as if he had never been away.

"So this is the beauty I've been hearing about and a bun in the oven to boot?" Billy 'Spud' Taylor slurred.

Val looked to Edith with a furrowed brow for guidance in the situation, but none was forthcoming. "And where is the useless pillock?" he continued.

"At work" Val simply replied, realising the less said the better.

"Ah, we're in agreement who we are talking about then, him in the fire brigade. That's a bloody laugh."

"Why?" Val had to speak out. This bully of a man was not going to have his own way.

"Chip off the old block, that's why; mark my words."

Again, looking at the terrified woman, Val decided it was up to her to rid the house of this drunken excuse for a man. Standing up, she went to the door and opened it then calmly spoke,

"We would like you to leave now." But he just sat in his old chair and smirked. Making a spluttering raspberry sound followed by a belch and a fart, he then spoke with spine chilling menace.

"You would like me to leave would you? This is my house. I'm not going anywhere."

"Leave now Mr Taylor or I am going to the phone box to ring the police." Val's voice portrayed a false calmness.

"And what are they going to do? It wouldn't be the first time that lot have been here with fingers up their arses, clueless the lot of 'em."

"Well, we'll see. Maybe they'll take action to protect a pregnant woman."

Then stumbling to his feet, he attempted to change his demeanour to old school charm.

"There's no need for that is there now, after all, we are practically family." And by placing his rough, calloused hands on her bump, the closeness of his stale alcohol and tobacco stench breath made her feel sick as he attempted to kiss her.

Raising her knee as high and hard as humanly possible in her condition, she grounded him with an agonising blow to his groin.

"Fucking bitch!" But he stopped short of retaliation when Edith came between them.

"Out! Once and for all!" Her new found courage took all by surprise, especially herself.

Turning his nose up in disbelief, he was again taken aback that he was no longer in control.

"I said OUT!" She reiterated in a way that was long, long overdue.

And with a pathetic sniff at the two women before him, he left with his proverbial tail between his legs.

And as for the two women, tears flowed as they embraced in relief at their temporary victory.

So is this it? Living in the spare room at Ray's mother's house; a single teardrop fell into her cup of tea. This is not the way it should be. Unmarried, more or less abandoned by her own parents, serious, serious doubts about her future, Valerie Sanderson's life was surely destined to be better than this.

In theory, they should have their own place by now. Two relatively good wages should pose no problem for a mortgage, but she felt that for some reason Ray was dragging his heels over the commitment. And where the bloody hell is he? He should have been home hours ago. His night shift finished at 9.00am. Then with an unnecessary twinge of guilt, she hoped he was ok, there could have been an accident at work or something? But what was something? She just didn't know; her head was all over the place. And what of the phone call she had made to the fire station to speak to him last week? The cagey reply had been, 'Oh, ...er Ray? He is out on a fire, they might be out for a while,' was more than a little suspicious.

"Oh girl, what have you done?" She asked herself. And standing to look at her reflection in the full length mirror, again tears fell. Her svelte like figure had been replaced by a huge bump that made her feel like a whale. "Pull yourself together!" she asserted. "Let's get this place finished, someone has to." And picking up the four inch paintbrush, she picked a hair off the bristles and wiped it on the bib of her yellow stained denim dungarees, before moving onwards if not necessarily upwards.

## Chapter 11

"Everything ok Ray?"
Blocky and Benny Bennett stood facing a flustered, breathless Ray at the out of town bus stop.

"Yeh," was Ray's somewhat vague reply.

"It's just that you only have one shoe on," Benny just happened to mention, with a look that bridged the gap between puzzlement and a humorous grin.

And looking to his foot, Ray casually uttered,

"Oh Yeh," as if this was, in some way, an explanation.

The standoff carried on for another minute or so, ending with the other two moving off when no rhyme or reason was forthcoming.

"What's all that about?" Ray could hear Blocky's fading words as they turned the corner.

He would have to act on his wits quicker than that in future, he reflected. Following his night shift, his plan was to enter the Hare and Hounds via the back door where an anticipant 'Big Joan' would be waiting, negligee clad. And all went to plan until Ron, her husband returned earlier than usual from the brewery accounts meeting, leaving him no time to fully re-dress.

Big Joan, an ample proportioned woman, twenty years his senior had taken Ray as her latest play thing. Her larger than life, south facing breasts would be unleashed upon her victims and in a playful almost motherly fashion their faces would be smothered in her cleavage by way of simplistic foreplay. Ray didn't actually know why he returned time after time to these ritualistic, mutual, self-gratification follies. But one thing was for sure; guilt would not be a contributory factor when time was eventually called on the out of hours' sessions. After all, if you're not getting it at home, get it where you can, is rule number one in 'Ray's law.

So, composure returned. The story of the missing shoe was finalised and the spring in his one-shoed step was back in abundance, as he grabbed the chrome bar of the open backed number eight bus.

Walking up the garden path of his and now their home, Rays confidence waned a little. Val was no fool, but if you get your story right and go over it in your head enough times, it is exactly the same as an actual memory, Ray convinced himself.

Edith Taylor watched her son through the spotlessly clean net curtains with a sense of inevitability. Yes, her offspring was turning into a young version of her useless husband. Feeling as though a clip around the ear hole was long overdue, she bit her lip and resisted. 'Don't get involved' she told herself. No one wants an interfering mother-in-law.

Bouncing up the stairs, Ray paused momentarily before opening the door to their home within a home.

"You ok?" He could see Val had been crying, but silence would be her only weapon in this war of wills on this occasion, for now at least. Feeling as though his explanation would fall upon deaf ears, he now felt off the hook. Hell, she wasn't even looking at his feet. However his inability to recognise real hurt would lead him to proverbially shoot himself in his exposed foot. Too good a story not to use, he continued with his fabrication none the less.

"Lost me shoe." He spoke in conjunction with waving his foot in small circular movements. Looking down, Val saw indeed he had only one shoe.

"Hmmm" was all she could muster.

"Fell out of the fire engine when we got to a fire last night." Still no reaction! "You know when we got changed into our wellies; it was on the floor and must have got kicked out in the rush."

"Hmmm." Val once again uttered the non-committal sound, she really couldn't be bothered being drawn in.

"So I've been back looking for it all morning, couldn't find it though."

Val could see holes in his story as big as the one in his sock, but would hang fire for a little longer.

"Right down near the gas works. I had to go back to."

Then, no longer able to resist, she casually mentioned, "Hop it?"

"What?" Ray's puzzled reply lamely hovered in the air.

"Did you hop it all the way?" Val put it to him.

"No I, well I did a bit, you know, walking more on one foot than the other." Waffle kicked in.

"Were those your only shoes? You get issued with more than one pair don't you?"

"Yeh, but I couldn't find them, must be here in the wardrobe." (Getting out an immediate response to this line of questioning pleased Ray.)

"Your wellies in the wardrobe too?"

"What do you mean?"

"Well if it was me, I would have worn them rather than walk without a shoe."

He was on the ropes and he knew it, but he couldn't back out now.

"We're not allowed to, against regulations and all that crap."

"What about the others, most of them drive don't they? Would one of them not give you a lift?"

"If you're gonna be like this then forget it; I mean a bit of trust wouldn't go amiss." Ray put on a hurt look in order to get some of the sympathy he stupidly imagined could be expected due to his plight.

"Ray."

"What?"

"Oh forget it!" What was the use? She resigned herself.

"No, go on, what is it?"

"If for one minute you think I'm going to put up with what your mother did for all those years, you have another think coming."

"Hey Sugar," Ray held out his hands.

"Sugar! Sweet! Honey! That stuff isn't going to work Ray, so one more slip up and I'm off, baby or no baby. Do you understand? This shit stops now or else."

"Yeh, but I think you are over reacting."

"Ray!" Val felt like screaming, what is it with him?

"Ok, ok, I know my place. What's for dinner? I'm starving," he shamefully enquired, lighting his cigarette as Val agonisingly rolled her eyes.

## Chapter 12 February 1966

Exactly why Val had agreed to meet Ray again was beyond her. These meetings had become an all too familiar routine. She held no reservations whatsoever that moving back to her parents home had been the right thing, so why should she listen to his apologies and bullshit anymore? Yes she had to let him see Thomas, but she would die before he could inflict any of his influences upon her son's impressionable young life.

She finally broke last summer. It wasn't the money missing from the purse, or the angry pub landlord at the door looking for Cinderella, or should I say Cinderfella, with a shoe in his hand. Although they were massive contributory factors, it was the slap. 'Only a slap' was how he put it, but the hard knuckle of the back of his hand broke her nose and blackened both her eyes. Of course she felt sorry for Mrs T and would not deny her access to her grandson, but only on neutral ground.

As for Ray, he couldn't quite figure out why his charm only had a fraction of that in its heyday. He was no different, so what had happened? Was it just possible that all those women who once smiled at him when he was together with Val, were doing so at the sight of a happy couple? Or had word spread around town of his cheeky wild days? Time would tell, but he sure didn't enjoy the prospect of a life full of 'Big Joans'. 'Shit, for Christ's sake, I am only twenty one years old, what am I doing with my life? Val will see sense, she has to. No one wants to bring up a sprog on their own; do they?'

Sat waiting in the San Remo cafe, Val was considering leaving. This latest meeting on Ray's request was already one person short. "Bloody late for his own funeral, he will be" she muttered. But almost as if sensing her frustration, he sprung through the door into the welcome warmth of the Italian/American style diner.

"Sorry I'm late, twenty bloody minutes I've waited for that bus." He shivered and turned his coat collar back down.

Val just held her hand up in a manner that signalled him to halt his words in their tracks. She had no stomach for his lame excuses right now. "Where's Tom?"

"He's with my mother, and it's Thomas."

The same tired old lady who served them on their first date returned to the exact same spot as she did on that fateful late evening. Was she permanently exhausted? Is that how she herself would look and feel one day?' she pondered.

"I want to see him." His sulky schoolboy look didn't appear to give rise to any prospect of maturity.

"You will do, we need to work out some kind of routine."

"On your terms I take it?"

"Yes, somewhere I know he is going to be safe."

"What you saying? That I'm going to hurt my own son."

"Look Ray, do you want to sort this out or not?"

"Yeh, but this is not just about you." There was bitterness in his voice.

"Right, what I propose is, that you or your mother pick him up on a Saturday or a Sunday, depending on your shift and bring him back later that same evening, at least until he's older."

"Wow! We are honoured aren't we?" he sarcastically remarked.

"Take it or leave it. It's that or court, you choose."

"Ok, for now, but one day I see us back together. I miss you." Val resisted saying 'you mean you miss a skivvy and your leg over,' but there was no point goading him. And as for any mention of love, well that would be way beyond him.

"Ray, we will never get back together, ever. Do you understand? What happened was a mistake and I intend to move on."

"So that's it? Got someone else already, have you?"

And closing her eyes, she slowly stood to leave. "And if you have, I'm not giving you any maintenance money." The childlike inner Ray returned.

"There's no one else, but when I'm ready to I'll make that decision."

"Yeh right, well, I'd grab him with both hands because nobody else will look at you with a kid in tow, you're used goods." Then almost with a sense of regret, he slightly lowered is head.

"Maybe not Ray, maybe no one will, but I'll take my chances."

Then leaving the booth and its occupant, she hoped to God she could break the chain of like-father-like-son, with nurture over nature.

**Chapter 13** **June 1969**

"Abso-fuckin-lutely, Yeh when?"

"Next Saturday. Are you ok with that, with work and all?" Terry enquired with his lopsided grin.

"Yeh, leave it with me. I'll sort it out, no problem."

"We'd have asked you before but we've not seen hide or hair of you for months; somebody said you were shacked up with Cleggy's wife."

"I was, but I've knocked it on the head. Looney tunes that one. Came off the pill so we could have a kid! Did she tell me? Did she bollocks!"

"Is she in the club?" Ian Turner asked with what appeared genuine concern.

"No, thank fuck, but I had a bit of a scare."

Ray had been asked to go to Pontins for a week; Charlie Cropper had dropped out under pressure from his girlfriend.

"I once went there as a youngster with me Mum and Dad," he fondly remembered. It was there he perfected the art of 'hand under armpit farting.' He'd made friends with a boy from Birmingham, what was his name? Anyway, the two of them had spent the whole week bare-chested, driving both sets of parents mad with the constant reproduction of noisy bum sounds.

Ray had also avoided this part of town, due to threats from the Brierley family. He should have known better than to mess around with their Linda. All interest had now been lost when she handed over her prize possession. How was he to know? She had always given the impression of 'an easy lay.' All talk she was, until his strong arm tactics in the bedroom. Only it wasn't the bedroom, it was at the back of the fishing lodges, while blokes cast their rods; he was doing similar, so to speak.

So he'd laid low for a while until the dust settled, but surely he couldn't be blamed for every lassies lack of moral virtues? And as for holiday romances, well they ask for everything they get.

## Chapter 14

"I thought we are all booked in, above board and all that?" Ray asked with a little concern.

"We are but, just act like a vicar's son or summat; all male parties aren't usually allowed."

"Why are you telling us this now?" Ray enquired further; he was annoyed at the lack of prior warning.

"My Mum knows someone at the booking office, and she's vouched for us; being goody-goodies and well behaved."

"Everything alright lads?" a burley security guard enquired at the gated entrance.

"We are sir" Terry politely answered.

"Are you booked in?" He peered through the open window at the occupants.

"Oh yes, the rest of our family have already gone in," he continued.

"Ok then, report first to the reception hall, drive along and its one hundred yards on the right."

"Thank you very much sir," he concluded his deceitful banter.

"You creeping git," Ray remarked, sniggering along with the others.

But the no nonsense security guard had their measure. He would be on the lookout for trouble from these four likely lads. And as for Ray, his day shift had begun that morning but he had booked in sick at work, 'well that can't do any harm can it?' was his firm belief.

"Did you see those lassies? I think they were Geordies; we've had the eye already."

"Is that all you think about?" Don was a little perplexed at Ray's apparent obsession with the ladies.

"Well what else are we gonna do except get pissed and trap off?" Ray incredulously stared at him.

"Yeh, we can do that, but we can go for a swim, watch the show, you know play it cool. Let 'em get a little frustrated by acting casual and nonchalant, and then they'll be beggin' for it!"

"Yeh Ray, let's play it down a bit," Terry backed him up. "And there's a comedian on tonight. I believe he's a cracker."

"Ok, ok," Ray held his hands up in defeat,"but don't blame me if they cop off with someone else."

"That wer' brilliant," Terry was still laughing from the memory of the comedian's stage performance.

"What was that one about the dog in the pub, I can never remember jokes," Ian added.

Taking a seat in the bar adjacent to the theatre, their joviality was on a natural high. Heavy barrelled beer glasses were placed in front of them by a busty brassy barmaid, who wasted no time by giving Ray a quick wink. And by returning the gesture, he felt sure holiday notch number one was already in the bag.

"Alright you lads, we've got you sussed." Stood looking over them were the Geordie girls they had seen at reception earlier.

"Sussed?" Terry enquired.

"Yeh, sussed out. You four have been acting all casual and uninterested, like you're pretending you haven't even noticed us." And for once they hadn't. Ray made a mental note, 'this may be the way forward after all.'

All four young men stood to greet the girls; at least some manners deep in their subconscious had been retained.

Ray held his hand out to the five girls and introduced the others,

"I'm Ray, this is Terry or fabric."

"Fabric?" a slightly plump mousey haired girl enquired.

"Yeh Fabric," Ray went on to explain, "He's called Terry Laine, sounds a bit like Terylene the material, so Fabric it is."

"Surely you could have come up with something better than that?" the apparent spokesperson of the girls asked.

"Maybe, it's either that or 'cloth ears' when he's not listening. And this is Ian, or sometimes Eddy."

"Go on, why?" another asked.

"Well it's Ian Turner or head turner, Eddy, get it?"

"Stomach turner, more like it... sorry no offence, it just rolled off me tongue," another remarked.

"No offence taken." Ian gave credit for the quick retort. To him, her vocal tone swayed along like poetry. A connection had already been made between him and the slim brunette.

"And this is Don, or nosey."

"Don't tell me, Donald Parker?"

"Yeh!" Ray was about to say, 'how do you know?' when he realised the girls were a lot sharper than he had given them credit for.

"I'm Dawn," the attractive girl, with the Twiggy style short bob hairstyle introduced herself. "And this is Sue," the plump mousey sort, returned a smile. "Sheila," the slim brunette, "and Jackie and Gilly," the two remaining as yet unspoken girls.

"Like the nursery rhyme" Don tried to impress in vain.

"No flies on you is there?" one or the other put him in his place immediately.

"And what do they call you Ray? What's your nickname?" Dawn tilted her head slightly to one side, as if searching into his eyes for an answer.

"It's just Ray, at least to my face it is."

"No, that's not good enough; I'll call you sunray, like I imagine your mother thinks shines out of your backside."

"Pphhr, if only you knew" Ray quickly quashed the idea.

"No I've got it, 'Sunny,' I'll call you Sunny."

As the evening came to a close, the live band that followed the comedian had in its turn been replaced by a DJ, rounding off the night with a selection of old and new tunes. Ray, Ian and Terry along with Dawn, Sheila and Sue had taken to the dance floor. Don however had bowed out to try and fathom out the other two. He knew which he would choose and who would be the gooseberry, but did they have other ideas, he just couldn't tell.

As the music slowed towards a midnight closure, Dawn and Ray moved together for a slow dance.

"Ah Sunny, I think your song is coming on."

"What do you mean?" Ray was a little puzzled.

"You're a good looking bloke, how many women have you been with? Five? Ten? Dozens? I'll bet dozens." Her line of questioning was in no way harsh or bitter; it was just her way of making him look at the person inside.

"Dunno, a few I suppose" Ray shrugged.

"Ahhh, modest hey?"

And after a slight pause, she quietly whispered a short sentence that would live with him for the rest of his life.

"Enjoy the music, but listen to the words Sunny, it may just be you."

And as he held her a little closer, he heard for the first time the haunting lyrics that to Ray would sadly echo far too many home truths. 'Man of the World' by Fleetwood Mac, softly concluded the evening's entertainment.

## Chapter 15

"Where the bloody hell is he?" Ian was a little concerned.

"Hey, you don't think he's copped for the two of 'em, do you?" Ray was a tiny bit jealous at the thought.

"What, tweedle dee and tweedle dum, or whatever they are called?" Terry popped up with an attempt at a humorous quip.

"Yeh, he was with them both last I saw of him."

Don hadn't staggered to bed the previous night with the others, now curiosity and speculation were in abundance.

"What if he's had an accident, maybe he went to the beach, the tides are notorious here." Ian was beginning to fret.

"He'll be alright, he's a big lad," Ray tried to reassure him. "Anyway I bet he's had one or the other, if not both, the jammy git!"

"No, I can't see Don with two birds at once, it just don't seem right." Terry shook his head as if to rid himself of the vision.

"Well there's only one way to find out what's happened, let's go and look for him" Terry announced authoritatively.

"Where do we begin?" Ray placed the first obstacle in the way of the search.

"The girl's chalet" Terry triumphantly sounded out.

"Where is it? They haven't told me." Ian looked to Ray as if he would be the fountain of knowledge in that department.

"Search me, I got nowhere with Dawn. I came home with you two, remember."

"Ok then let's just go and have a look around for him, it's a start at least." Terry held out his hands as if to signal the only option available to them, is to go and physically search for their friend.

The vast grounds of the holiday camp revealed nothing of Don, along with the immediate beach area. It was lunchtime before it was Ray who was proved correct, well sort of.

Totally oblivious to the kerfuffle he'd caused, he was spotted heading for his midday meal, linked on either side by the two Geordie girls.

"What did I tell you? Look, he's got both of them on his arm" Ray smugly announced.

"Well I'm gonna find out what's happened." Ian went off in pursuit of the threesome.

"See you later Don, we'll do it again tonight if you like?" Jackie fondly waved him goodbye as they parted to go to their respective, allocated dining tables.

"Bloody hell Don, you're a dark horse," Ray in a congratulatory way caught up with him, in front of Ian. "What did I say?" he reiterated as the others joined them.

"Where have you been?" Terry enquired.

"When?" Don innocently replied.

"Last night; all night, all morning, when do you think?" Ray egged him on for information.

"Oh right, you mean with the girls?"

"Yeh, with the girls, Dumbo! What else would we mean?" Ray prompted.

"Down the beach," was Don's simple reply.

"What did I tell you?" Ray again delighted in his assumption.

"Whereabouts? We looked along the beach for you," Ian offered.

"We walked for about a mile or two down, then we lit a camp fire and philosophised."

"What?" Ray couldn't believe his ears, "You took two birds down the beach, lit a fire and philosophised?"

"Yeh, we talked about the universe. Did you know there are more stars in the universe than grains of sand on all the beaches and deserts on earth?"

"Yeh, but did any get in awkward places?" Ray made light of the deep and meaningful topic.

"It's true, and we talked of life on other planets; it's a given."

"Bollocks," Ray again couldn't manage to rise to a higher level of conversation.

"Some of the stars we can see are already extinct. The light takes so long to get here, they have died out ages ago," Don persisted none the less. "You know next month, the Americans intend to put a man on the moon. In the vastness of space, that's no distance at all." He held his thumb and forefinger a fraction apart as to illustrate his meaning.

"I know what his wife will say when he gets back," and pausing for effect before continuing, Ray finished his pun. "Where on earth have you been? Do you get it? Where on earth! Oh forget it." His joke fell on deaf ears.

"Then we tried our hand at transcendental meditation."

"What?" Ray again spoke with incredulity.

"You know, Yoga like the Beatles' Guru introduced."

Shaking his head, Ray decided enough was enough.

"Two birds on the beach, a hot summer's night, and you do yoga!"

"Yeh that's right," Don casually continued. "We totally relaxed our bodies, then had mind blowing, free and uninhibited sex." His voice tailed off so quietly at the end of his sentence, the others almost missed it.

"What?" All three squealed in unison.

"Yeh, but it wasn't about the sex, it was the emancipation and liberation of our inner selfs'."

"I knew it, I knew it, I knew it!" Ray at last claimed victory.

"You don't get it, do you Ray?"

"Not yet I don't, but I will when we all go down the beach tonight." He was almost dancing on the spot at the prospect.

"It doesn't happen like that; you just want to go and bonk your brains out. That's not what it's all about." Don shook his head at the thought.

"Maybe not for you, but I intend to do just that."

"I'd rather not go again than it turn into some kind of orgy."

"Leave him to it Ray," Terry broke in. "It's his thing, let them get on with it, we've got the others to do our thing with."

"Yeh, leave him be." Ian supported Terry's intervention.

"Ok, but if they can put a word in for us with the other three, I'd be grateful." Ray still imagined all five girls as free-love hippy chicks, dancing naked around a camp fire.

His trance was broken by a Hungry Terry, nodding his head towards the dining room.

"Come on, I'm starving." And off to dine went the four fair-weather friends, with a spring in their steps.

## Chapter 16

To say Ray was a little perplexed would be an understatement. Worried would probably be more appropriate. Was he losing his touch, or worse still, his looks? All the others it would seem had broken their holiday duck, although Don neither knew of, nor cared about any challenges. They in all honesty, only really existed in Ray's head, so his own problem was now paramount.

He and Dawn had paired off as a couple, but for only the second time in his life, someone had got his measure and been accepted as an equal. At least that's what he was admitting to in his subconscious mind. In all honesty, he was besotted; to Ray she was perfect. They had hit it off immediately, compatible in every way, but she just didn't appear to be ready to jump into the sack. They had kissed; he had held her close, but any cheap moves he had intended, somehow he now refrained from. He had similar feelings with Val, but this was at a different level altogether. 'Is this how people get caught up in holiday romances?' he asked himself. But his main concern now was, tomorrow they will part and go their different ways.

How would he confront the situation? He didn't know. Not at any point in his life had he ever uttered the 'L word'. Not to his mother, his son and definitely not to any of his many conquests. He couldn't bear the thought of never seeing her again, so some action, at some point would be necessary.

As the four applied their finishing touches, elbow room around the mirror was in short supply. Combs flicked the very different hairstyles into place and a last dab of aftershave was absorbed into their clean-shaven faces.

Ray now knew what a man condemned to the gallows would experience. He felt that after tonight, his life might come to an end. He fully understood the analogy was somewhat exaggerated, but none the less the similarity was firmly in place.

"Where the hell did that week go?" Terry shook his head at how the time had flown.

"Tell me about it, but what a week hey?" Ian added.

But all four agreed, for whatever their own personal reasons, this was one week to remember.

Ian and Terry, it would appear took the holiday for what it was, a good time while it lasted. But Ray and Don, for totally different reasons were not ready to call time just yet.

"What is it Sunny?" The gangs had been huddled around two tables in the bar and only now had he and Dawn been left alone. But for once, Ray couldn't find any words; he just soulfully gazed into Dawn's deep blue eyes. "You've been looking at your watch all night, what is it?"

It was true, he had been clockwatching all evening, in a vain effort to try and slow it down. "This isn't what I think it is, is it Sunny?" Dawn asked.

"What do you mean?" Ray tried to harden his act.

"Nar nothing... It's just that you look like... ah forget it." Dawn was unable to say what was really on her mind.

Taking hold of her hand, Ray hoped his actions would replace the need for words, three words in particular.

"We've had a good time haven't we? I mean this week has been brilliant hasn't it?" Ray finally found his tongue.

"Oh Yeh, absolutely fantastic."

"I would like to... er do you think that, there is any chance we might meet up again sometime?"

"Ray, is this a ploy to try and bed me? If so, that brassy barmaid that has had her eye on you all week, might be an easier option."

"What, no way, it's you I want to be with, I, I, I er really like you."

"I like you too Sunny, but we are just friends aren't we?"

"Yeh but I think I..." but the words would not surface.

"Ray, Sunny, I can't see you again; there's a reason but I don't want to talk about it."

"Is there someone else?"

"Like I said, I don't want to talk about it; can we just enjoy the last of the evening like good friends?"

Ray felt like someone had physically kicked him in the stomach and again he searched her eyes.

"Hey Sunny, that's not a...?" but stopped short in her words so as not to embarrass him.

"Nar, what me? No chance." He wished the damp mist in his eyes would dry up without having to wipe it away.

"Come on Sunny, last half hour, let's go and dance."

So with feet that felt like lead and a smile so false it belonged in Madame Toussauds, he saw the evening out with someone he had now been told twice was 'just a friend'.

## Chapter 17

"Ah, Mr Taylor, come on in and take a seat."
Ray's first day back at work was initially started with a heavy heart, but it was about to get worse. He had been summoned to the offices of the fire brigade hierarchy.

He had already filled in the paperwork surrounding his absence from work, so what all this was about was anyone's guess. He had witnessed many people take time off sick and just filled in a report and that was the end of it. And what was this 'Mr Taylor' business? The big family brotherhood which is the fire service does not stand on ceremony for no reason.

As he took a seat opposite 'chrome dome,' one of the more senior officers, he once again marvelled at the sight of his shiny head. Perfect in proportion, it was not unlike a small Chinese wok. But moreover, it was the smoothest polished scalp known to man. He had a vision of his wife buffing it up every morning before he left for work.

A hand to mouth cough had the effect of returning Ray to the proceedings in question.

"Ok let's get to the point, it says here, in not too good English that you have suffered some sort of stomach disorder?" and Ray's own hand written report was pushed under his nose.

'Reason for absence: *diohre gastroint* the runs.'

"Yes that's right." Ray's theory was to say as little as possible to avoid tripping himself up.

"So it appears that you possess neither a dictionary nor a doctor's note, is that a correct assumption?"

"Well I didn't think I needed one."

"I think both would be a good idea for future reference, but I digress. So, how are you feeling now?"

"Not too bad." Still keeping it simple.

"Sea air do you good, did it?"

Ray felt like a rabbit caught in the headlights, how did he know?

"Cat got your tongue?" Chrome dome leaned a little closer to him across the table.

"I just er, needed some, er, you know" Ray spluttered.

And holding his hand up, to summon him to stop, he took control of what Ray now realised was a disciplinary hearing.

"You were seen at a certain holiday camp last week in what appears to be good health."

"Seen?" Ray said with some surprise.

"Yes, seen. So wrapped up in your own little world, you failed to notice someone, who will remain nameless, legitimately taking their summer vacation.

"I've been grassed up?" he muttered under his breath.

"I prefer to say that your stupid folly has been uncovered."

"So right, to the point, I am to assume you do not deny anything that I have put to you?"

"I don't think there would be any point would there." Ray resigned himself to his fate.

"Well I have no option then but to issue you with a written warning," and looking to the other officer present at the disciplinary, a firm nod of the head was the only acknowledgement offered. "Ok this meeting is now concluded, so everything said now is off the record."

"Yes," Ray replied with more than a little numbness.

"Ray, we look after our own within the fire service, as you know. But the line has definitely got to be toed. If you persist with this 'chap around town' character, another less disciplined vocation may be more suited to your persona." The gentleman that Ray liked and even admired, returned. The soft, warm tones of his superior now felt like firm fatherly advice, rather than a stern bollocking.

"Yes sir. I will take on board everything said."

"Good, that's good Raymond. Now return to your duties and keep your nose clean."

"Phew." Ray's relief was evident as he closed the door behind him. "Shit, I thought I was going to get sacked" he muttered to himself as he returned to the sanctuary of fire station life, but who, he frowned at the thought, who had spotted him?"

**Chapter 18**

What is it with you Ray?" Barry was searching for clues as to why Ray had been summonsed upstairs.

"Nowt." Ray felt like he was being dragged deeper into some type of depressive state.

"You were like this even before chromo wanted to see you. You've not been kicked into touch by some bird have you?" Barry couldn't fathom Ray's silent stare that replaced any verbal reply.

"Chromo invite you round for a dinner date with his daughter?" Barry tried to lighten the atmosphere a little.

But Ray wasn't in the mood for any kind of banter or indeed interrogation. It would all come out in the wash when his new immediate officer in charge read the disciplinary report. Discretion was not one of his qualities and his fondness for Ray, non-existent.

Stepping outside, his deep intake of fresh air was followed by an equally long drag on his cigarette. He felt drained. He wished he could just go to sleep and make it all go away. But he knew it wouldn't. If he could see Dawn once more in a different environment, he was sure he could win her round.

So what were his options? Jump on a train and go find her or ride out the emotional storm and do nothing? He didn't even have her address, due to the nature of their final parting. He felt that asking would have been seen as a weakness.

"Stupid pillock, you stupid stubborn pillock!" he said a little too loud to himself and looking around, he was slightly relieved to see no one was in earshot.

Stubbing out his cigarette with his foot, he returned indoors to admit his guilt to his colleagues. There was no point in trying to hide that aspect of his problems, they would find out anyway, so it may as well come from the horse's mouth. As for Dawn, he had thought of a plan which might just work.

Moodily joining the others at the dining table, he took his usual seat and holding his hand up so as to admit the misdemeanour already being speculated, he began a difficult confession. But no sooner had he opened his spiel, when the fire station alarm cut it short. Cheers erupted from certain quarters as only one of the two engines was to be dispatched due to the call out only being a rubbish fire, thus leaving half the team to finish their midday meals with smiles on their faces.

Ray couldn't care less about the food, which was so far untouched. Even before these latest two knocks, many meals had been replaced with liquid lunches, so this one was just another drop in the ocean.

"Whoa, slow down!" Dave Ball, a fire-fighter of many years experience shouted from the rear cab to the front. But Arthur Mann only knew two speeds when driving to fires, fast and extremely fast. Dave muttered, "absolutely stupid, driving to a rubbish fire like this, he'll kill somebody one day." Then almost as if a premonition, the inevitable seemed destined to unfold.

Swerving to miss a cyclist on a blind bend, they clipped the kerb ending on the wrong side of the road. The unforgiving dry stone wall then began to unravel the side of the appliance, like a can opener would a tin of sardines. The exposing of the internal workings of the engine only ceased when a stone terrace gable-end abruptly intervened.

On a scale of injuries, Ray's lay mid division. Arthur had driven to his last fire, a fractured skull, broken pelvis and shattered legs would see to that. Inconclusive head injuries, a broken arm and ribs had the effect of sending Bernie Ibbotson into the offices of the fire prevention department. Dave Ball and Barry Carter suffered minor fractures and cuts and bruises.

Ray awoke in a hospital bed the following day. Having suffered concussion, a broken arm and collar bone and facial injuries, not in any way extreme disfigurement but just enough to imagine his venture into the boxing ring had been longer lived.

Last year he had been persuaded to take up the pugilistic pastime and enter some minor tournaments. Three fights later he decided to throw in the towel, when he overheard his new nickname was to be 'cauliflower arse' due to the amount of time his backside was canvas bound.

"How are you today Raymond?"

"Oh please, you sound like my mother, just Ray."

"Are you feeling any better Ray?" asked a pretty, young nurse by the name of Andrea Connell, if her name tag was to be believed. "Your friend Arthur gave us a bit of a scare but it seems you'll all live."

"Was anyone else involved in the crash?" Ray asked tentatively.

"No. Thankfully the people in the house were out at the time."

"What about the cyclist?"

"I don't know of any cyclist, so he mustn't have been involved. Oh I nearly forgot; you've had visitors."

Ray had some stupid notion that it might have been Dawn; heard through the grapevine or a newspaper report and rushed to be at his bedside. However the description fitted his mother and Thomas. Then his selective guilt resurfaced. When was the last time he had taken his son out, or even seen him? He just wasn't paternal, he knew that, but he would put it right, he vaguely promised himself.

But Ray's shameful self-confessions were interrupted by more visitors.

"Ah Ray, good to see you back with us."

Chrome dome and his entourage gathered around his bed.

"Dave Ball and Barry Carter have been discharged, but I'm afraid Arthur may be hospitalised for some time." He was almost apologetic in his manner that he'd had cause to discipline Ray earlier; that was the nature of the gentleman officer.

"The doctor says Bernie and you are making good progress, but you take your time with your recovery."

'Don't worry I will' Ray thought to himself, but the words which actually left his lips were those of, "Thank you, I can't wait to get back."

"That's good Ray, let's forget the past and look forward to a bright future."

Ray managed an injured small boy nod in recognition and closed his eyes to emphasise his need for recuperative respite.

"Right come on, we must leave Mr Taylor to his recovery." Behind closed eyes, he listened to the movement of the bedside gathering shuffle away until he finally breathed a sigh of relief.

"A cup of tea, Ray?" Andrea approached with a cheeky smile on her face.

"Oh yes," and with a grin that really should be beyond his suffering, he added, "that would be perfect."

**Chapter 19** **September 1969**

Pooch walking aside, Ray marvelled at how dramatically his fortunes could change for the better. Three major body blows earlier in the summer and now, with the exception of Andrea's white, curly haired poodle, his life was back on track; well sort of!

Sitting on a bench in the newly re-christened 'Mandy Moon Park', he held a neatly folded piece of paper between his fingers.

Recently sculpted to compliment the upmarket housing estate, a large landscaped area lay adjacent to the overpriced development. Due to recent global and cosmic events, the planned mock countryside feature undertook some last minute changes.

The small central lake was now surrounded by a crescent shaped path. So should anyone be fortunate enough to have an aerial view, a quarter moon shaped gravel walkway would be visible. Thousands of shrubs and sapling trees were planted in the several acre site. It now also featured the addition of a raised observation area, where if so inclined, one could look to the heavens and stargaze.

The date of the first moon landing, over the evenings of 20th to 21st July was firmly etched on Ray's memory. It was then that he moved his entire belongings (one suitcase,) from a back bedroom at Blocky's Mum's run-down terrace, to the relative splendour of Doctor Felix White's Victorian detached property.

"Dr White," he had a little chuckle to himself. And a memory returned of his mother sending him to the corner shop with a hastily scribbled note, only to return with a soft package placed in a brown paper bag.

Digression aside, Andrea had persuaded the said doctor to rent out the final room at the house, usually reserved for nurses, to Ray.

"Well he is part of the emergency services." She had finally twisted his arm, in opposition to his usually canny decision making.

So in his first evening, Ray and his four new female friends settled down in the communal living area, to watch the television coverage of Neil Armstrong, Buzz Aldrin and Michael Collins making history.

'Mateus Rose' was flowing in abundance and by his observation of the amount of candle bearing, wax stained empties, this favourite of the girls was consumed in enormous proportions.

And by making a previously heard conversation his own, he attempted to move the level up a notch by copying Don's actions of placing his thumb and finger a fraction apart he then began his version.

"In the great scheme of things, this moon journey is like nothing, zilch, a gnat's willy size in terms of space travel." A drunken giggle from the girls gave him further encouragement. "Did you know that there are more grains of sand on earth than stars in the sky?"

"Well I can believe that, if you think of all the deserts and beaches." Karen, Ray's least likely potential conquest amongst the girls, considered.

"Wait a minute," Julie, the complete opposite, cut in, "isn't that the other way around? More stars than sand on earth?"

"That's what I said isn't it?" Ray tried to cover his lack of knowledge on the subject with humour.

"You're not behind the door are you Ray?" Andrea joined in.

"Up there for thinking, down there for dancing," he pointed from his head to his feet, simultaneously grinning from ear to ear.

As the small hours approached, Debbie or Debs as she insisted upon being called had already succumbed to sleep.

"When's it gonna happen?" Andrea yawned.

"Depends what you mean," Ray cheekily speculated.

"I mean, how you gonna keep me awake so I can tell my grandchildren how I witnessed the first man land on the moon?"

So sneaking off on discovery, the other two had also given way to slumber; the much anticipated event was missed due to their own 'out of this world' experience.

Unfolding the piece of paper, he read again the information jotted down in Don's handwriting. Decisions, decisions! Maybe a pint down the White Lion would give some clarification. But this time he must remember not to leave snowy the dog tied up outside when leaving for home!

"Right come on, let's go," he instructed his unlikely canine companion and passing the newly graffiti-defaced sign at the gated entrance, he could still read the official lettering underneath, 'Man o' the Moon Park, opened July 1969.'

**Chapter 20** **October 1969**

'If it ain't broke, don't fix it.' How many times had Ray heard that saying? It was also one of his own motto's, along with, 'why do today what you can put off 'til tomorrow?' So what on earth was he doing? He'd started off on this journey last week, only to turn back at the last minute, but this time he had actually boarded the Newcastle bound train. Yes, he was to change at Leeds, maybe he should back out there? But, as for now, he was closing in on the address in Ponteland supplied by his friend. 'What kind of place name was that anyway?' he wondered. He had a vision of Disneyland crossed with Pontins.

'Why am I doing this? I live in every single man's dream home' he asked himself again. Andrea if not his girlfriend was a willing on/off bed partner. Debs and Karen a definite no, no! But Julie he felt would follow Andrea's lead eventually, if the flirting was any guide. When the two girls were on different shifts, Ray would chance his arm at least with Julie. So what was the lure? Quite simply, he could not get the memory of his short time spent with Dawn out of his head. 'You'll get there and find she has a boyfriend or even a husband,' he told himself and if not, what his ultimate goal was, still confounded him.

Passing rows and rows of terraced houses that looked destined for demolition, Ray lit a cigarette on board his vantage point, which headed ever closer to his destination. Sat on the top deck of the bus inching north from the city centre, he reflected on how life would be so much easier if he could drive. 'Why don't you drive Ray?' How many times had he heard people ask? 'Nah, not for me' would be his simple reply and hope that would be the end of it, but it was something else deep within his psyche that affected that aspect of his life. Quite simply, it scared him, not the crash or any other physical event; it was the fear of failure. He had taken a couple of lessons, but his coordination was terrible. Trying to make his feet do something while his hands did another in conjunction with reading the road ahead, was completely alien to Ray. 'Don't worry Ray, it's the same for everyone, it will all come together,' he could still hear the words of his driving instructor. But Ray just knew that when he went off after work, to home or wherever he took himself, he would be laughing at Ray's inabilities. Sniggering behind his back, 'that bloody Ray Taylor, he's useless.'

He would sometimes come across similar situations in life, especially at work. Not always, but at times he might walk into a room and it would fall silent. Or he might catch the end of a sentence possibly directed at him. For these sorts of things he would always have to be on his guard. 'Acting the goat' his mother would say, or 'class clown,' likewise his teachers, but these traits had the effect of deflecting any negative views towards him, he found.

As the slums with their weekly washes hung out for public viewing were replaced with a more rural outlook, Ray shook his dark thoughts away.

The nerves that replaced his paranoia were good, he told himself. They would sharpen his wits in what was sure to be a tricky situation. This was his domain, one-to-ones with the opposite sex, mainly came out in his favour. Still Dawn was no ordinary woman; no one knew that more than he. No other woman would have brought him all this way; that was for sure.

Unfolding the piece of paper for the umpteenth time, he could almost smell her perfume; no that in itself was too simplistic, it was her whole presence, shampoo, fabric conditioner it was... well it was Dawn.

Imagining he was a private detective standing by the lamppost on the tree-lined bungalow avenue, he waited for his big entrance; however his hesitation in diving straight in could either be described as a blessing or fate.

As qualities go, or rather lack of them, shallowness is up near the top of Ray's failings. He of all people would admit to that, but at this one moment in his life, it made him feel ashamed of himself.

He took a deep breath when the front door of her house was suddenly brashly flung open. Had she seen him? Was she rushing to jump into his arms as in some black and white movie, maybe like the one set on a railway station? He could hear her soft voice, albeit a little flustered and hurried,

"Come on or we'll be late."

The sharp movement of her arm instructed someone out from the doorway. Then hands on hips in a stern motherly way, her impatience grew.

To Ray, what unfolded was a complete body blow. The sulky stomp of a small red haired boy would normally be enough to send him packing, but instantly he knew he would not be able to handle a life with Dawn. Perhaps four or five years old, the child being ushered into the red mini was downs-syndrome.

Perhaps he could instantly mature and embrace them as a family, putting aside the fact that Dawn hadn't even ever expressed a desire to see him again. But way beneath his skin-deep exterior, he knew it could never be.

Turning his back to avoid recognition, the ageing tiny car spluttered into action and quickly sped past him. Once again, this woman unwittingly made his eyes sting, but his acknowledgement of his own capabilities was a painful step forward towards understanding his own limitations.

**Chapter 21** **August 1972**

"A bloke?"

"He's a male nurse Ray and yes, he's moving in."

Ray was aghast; a fella as a nurse, whatever next, women in the fire brigade? But he could rest in the knowledge that would never happen.

"It's called equal opportunities and he's very welcome." Andrea was not to be fazed in her defence of Lance.

"Yeh, but come on, I mean..." still lost for words, he had a vision of Kenneth Cope dressed as a nurse in one of the carry on films.

"Oh and while I remember, Felix needs to talk to you about the rent" Andrea added.

Ray wondered when that would rear its ugly head again. Paying the rent was a bit of an inconvenience; it has the effect of chipping into his disposable income (beer money). By his own calculations he had made seven of the last twelve monthly payments, surely that wasn't too bad?

These days though, he felt the good time era of the house had gone. His brief affair with Andrea lasted only a few weeks and his intended next conquest, that being Julie, never materialised. The others had moved on, being replaced several times by new occupants, but never a man before!

The tide it seems has turned against him once more. His presence more tolerated than embraced, maybe it was something to do with his love of the tour of local pubs. When not working, his departure at 7.00pm prompt would then see his return, perhaps one hour after closing. This might entail good humoured banter, sometimes attempted gropes or more often than not, a paralytic crash out.

As the bell would ring at last orders for the night, he and the other die-hards would scramble to purchase two or even three pints to fuel their need to consume a sufficient tally. His circuit of hostelries for the evening would perhaps have been half a dozen and his latest tales of entertainment would be of his antics within the nurses' accommodation. Some loosely based on truth, but the majority fiction, would none the less be detailed as actual events. Mixed in with his jokes, tried and tested around the venues, should the listeners be in the same place twice, déjà vu would 'once again' be evident.

"Did I tell you when one of the girls gave me an injection? She said, 'just a small prick.' I said how do you know?" Ray slurred.

"Yeh Ray, we've heard that one" Benny Bennett yawned.

"Well what about when she said, 'have a go with my stethoscope and test my heart,' so I said big breaths, and her reply was, 'yeth and I'm only thixteen.'" Ray exaggerated a girls' lisp for effect.

"Yeh Ray, we've seen the film" another chipped in.

But the sanctuary of the Bar is preferable to the loneliness of his sparsely furnished room. There, dark thoughts would return, ever more so since the latest developments. Part of this month's rent money had been used to buy himself back into Thomas' life. A second-hand, but even so, good condition blue chopper bike, only to find that stepdad, Julian Bloody

Wilks-Lodge, of Frome, Wilding & Wilks-Lodge solicitors, had only gone and bought him a brand new red one!

Married last month, a stupid double-barrel name would suit Val right down to the ground, or is it now to be treble? Valerie Sanderson-Wilks-Lodge he bitterly wondered. Her exams now passed, she could now join the firm to take up position fleecing the public with their extortionate fees.

"Ah well, I might need one someday, maybe I might get a discount for old time's sake," but the bitter and twisted words left a sour taste in his mouth.

## Chapter 22

In no way was work going to interfere with the bank holiday festivities. He should surely have learned his lesson but old habits die hard, it seemed. His night shift clashed with the afternoon fun day activities at the Pack Horse. The rural pub had been granted a special afternoon licence due to its charity fund-raising. "Licensing laws," Ray scoffed, these technicalities would more often than not ruin a good session, by closing mid-afternoon. But today was an exception, the forward thinking landlord saw a loophole and was going to exploit it to the max.

And word was spreading fast that this out of the way watering hole was to stay open all day. Virtually unheard of, legally at least, it was a magnet for hardened drinkers for miles around. Ray cursed his luck that he was to work on this auspicious occasion.

Clarkey, his lift to the scene of the alcohol frenzy, was ten minutes late. "Valuable supping time being wasted," he muttered to himself. His plan was to pace himself through the afternoon, then freshen himself up a little, before keeping his head down at work. It wasn't totally unheard of for him or even some of the others to have the odd snifter before work. So what harm is there? He convinced himself.

Pacing up and down in conjunction with looking up and down the street for his latest buddy, he realised he'd got to 12.10pm before his daily thought of Dawn had surfaced. Not one day had passed without his still aching heart, memorising or fantasising about this one woman. It was usually first thing in the morning or last thing at night, but none the less, she was never far from his thoughts.

"Thank God for that!" He had almost worn the carpet threadbare by his movements whilst waiting. "About time!" and springing from his front door he jumped into the clapped out 'Hillman Hunter.'

"Bloody hell Clarkey, I thought you weren't coming," and lifting the car door back into place, due to the rotting of its hinges, he sank into the collapsing faux leather seat.

"Had to take me Mum to me aunties," he lamely replied in his almost childlike tones.

Looking around the car's interior, Ray remarked

"When was the last time you cleaned it out?

"'Ant ever cleaned it out," his answer not even childlike, more docile.

"I can tell." Ray, no domestic god himself, was shocked at the mess. Cigarette packets, sweet wrappers, newspapers, but most disturbing of all, four dead rabbits! Then looking down, Ray remarked in a puzzled manner, "Clarkey, there's mushrooms growing in the carpet!"

"Yeh, floors knackered; leaks like buggery."

Winding down the window Ray thought 'to each his own, the dirty bastard!'

"Take it you still go shooting" Ray nodded towards the back seat.

"'Ant had time to gut 'n' skin 'em yet, want one?"

"Think I'll give it a miss, but thanks for the offer."

"Anytime."

Then the journey descended into silence. It's a good job Clarkey isn't on the telly Ray thought; he's so far behind, he'd fall out of the back.

Bunting, cake stalls, tombola and various tents awaiting investigation were on display as they approached the venue, but these were just incidentals as far as Ray was concerned. The car park, already full left them with a short walk from the nearby field now being used for overspill parking.

The place was heaving and Ray was itching, not from the car, but itching to get into the bar. Already four deep, his irritability would normally have to be suppressed, at least until his turn, but these stupid temporary barmaids didn't have a clue who to serve next. So peering over numerous heads, he managed to catch one particular girl's eye. "Two pints of bitter," he called out and was promptly served. But unbeknown to Ray two pairs of the shoulders he had successfully bypassed, belonged to Alan and John Brierley. They were two of the brothers of a seven strong family, who even before today, had a particular hatred for Ray and quietly observed his impatience.

He needn't have bothered about his night shift; it was never to happen for Ray at least. Biding their time, the Brierley brothers caught up with Ray when he took his relief behind one of the beer tents.

His ribs cracked to the sound of the brass band playing 'The Liberty Bell,' more commonly known as the theme tune to Monty Pythons Flying Circus. Only needing the smallest excuse to catch up with Ray, Alan and John left him with a broken nose along with internal injuries. The last memory of that afternoon was of laughter from the revellers, along with one almighty raspberry at the tunes conclusion.

The phone call to work, two hours into his shift ended some speculation at least. Most money was on 'pissed up at some birds flat', but they could now officially put his absence down to an off-duty injury. Opinions of Ray split his colleagues; half thought his antics highly amusing, the rest a waste of space. But whatever their views, almost everyone wished him no harm.

However, only two people took the trouble to visit Ray the following day, divisional officer Steel and his assistant Mike Naylor. The retirement of 'chrome dome' last year saw the aptly named Richard Steel take his place. Not one to suffer fools gladly, he had Ray's measure.

Following a consultation with one of the doctors, he understood he would have, all being well, turned in for work with an enormous amount of alcohol in his system.

"Mr Taylor, come and see me when you're well enough to return to work, I think we need to talk." Steel's icy words left him cold.

"Here we go again," Ray shivered as the frosty words circulated around his brain.

**Chapter 23** **December 1972**

"Take it or leave it Ray, it makes no difference to me." Alf Reed had offered him accommodation in the scrap yard caravan for a small rent, payable in advance of course. In hindsight he did have another option, but sometimes the simplest of solutions are the hardest to see. His eviction from his latest digs had left him homeless and as a result he felt, left with no choice.

The vision of the hovel would live with him for the rest of his life; filthy, cold, no not cold, freezing! It was not living, it was dossing. Looking at his reflection in the cracked mottled mirror, he barely recognised himself, through the dirt and brown patches that lurked within the glass itself, a gaunt, poorly-looking ghost stared back at him.

For the first time in his life he found the need to use a belt to hold his trousers up. With a penknife he had from his brief days as a boy scout, along with cutting his finger; he made another tighter notch in order to make it fit for use. These days he would more often than not, go into work early, his entry could almost be classed as sneaking in. He would try and creep in unspotted, so he could take a warm shower and try to make himself respectable. Once or twice his appearance had been commented on and this along with his second written warning left him on stony ground. Steel had mercilessly issued the bollocking along with a copy of the charges, on his return from his last hospitalisation. But most disturbing of all, on one of his early slopes into the station, temptation nearly got the better of him. Finding himself alone when the day shift had turned out to a fire, he found sanctuary in the kitchen mess area. Opening the communal fridge, he discovered a hefty homemade plate meat pie. He was starving and taking hold of the weighty meal, he was about to tuck in when he grabbed hold of his senses,

"What are you doing stealing from your colleagues, what have you come to?" And placing it back on the shelf, he was shocked at what he had almost done. "You're many things Ray Taylor, a womaniser, a drunk and sometimes a complete idiot, but one thing you're not is a thief."

It was at this moment he realised the obvious. After his shift tonight, the last before going on leave, he would hopefully return home.

In doing so, it would have been too much to hope for, for there to be no questions asked. And indeed his mother made clear her intentions, by making a no nonsense list of conditions attached to the new beginning. Whether or not she believed her good for nothing son; his tears proved the old proverb of 'blood being thicker than water', somewhat profoundly relevant.

But if truth be known, Edith Taylor was secretly a little relieved to have a male presence back under her roof. Only time would tell if her only offspring could ever change his spots though.

**Chapter 24** **August 1976**

"Oh no, I don't like him; he's too daft to laugh at. I prefer them three making silly inventions in the countryside."

Ray would never have believed that he would now be sitting down with a cup of tea and watching television with his mother.

"Oh look! That would never happen!" She tutted at the manic episode of Fawlty Towers. But all the same, out of the corner of his eye, he caught her laughing as the sight of Basil Fawlty goose-stepping around, finally sparked a chuckle.

"Is that window still open? It's sweltering in here."

"Yes and the back door," Ray once again assured her. And picking up her Spanish fan that her sister Florrie had brought her back from Lloret-de-Mar, she wearily tried to cool herself.

The stifling temperatures had sapped Ray's energy too. Work was gruelling due to the heat-wave that looked set to continue. Stretched to the limit, the fire service had every appliance working around the clock to dampen down the moorland fires, as well as their usual workload. He would arrive at work in the morning pick up his packed lunch and if he was lucky, return home two or three hours after his shift would normally have finished.

But he was happy, happier than he had been for a long time. Life was... Well life was ordinary; no ups and no spiralling downs. Occasional girlfriends, nothing special and a limited social life down the pubs and clubs. Too much to ask to cut that aspect of his life totally out, but a steady two or three nights was appropriate for his bachelor status. More importantly though; a truce had developed between him and the management, along with one with Val and Thomas.

"You're a little old to still be living with your mother," the pretty Beverley Curzon was bombarding him with endless personal questions.

"I suppose so, but it suits" Ray simply replied.

The two of them had crossed paths earlier that day. As he and three of the others had taken a break from the grass beating to extinguish the flames of a burning field. The slender, blond, eighteen year old had brought to them welcome refreshments in the shape of homemade iced lemonade. Living at the farm that lay adjacent to the blaze, the prospect of four men in the vicinity was too good an opportunity to miss. Not backward in coming forward, she had eventually singled out Ray to direct her attentions at. With faces that were charcoal black, eyes, noses and mouths taking the brunt of the smoke, Ray wondered how she made her decision to single him out.

But ask him out she did and here they were in the popular Coach and Horses public house.

"I'm surprised you're not married or taken for, you scrub up quite well." Beverley held Ray's gaze in a way that would never leave her described as a wall flower.

"No, neither married or dating, the single life for me," Ray proudly stated.

"Well, we'll see if we can't change that." Beverley's immediate reply would have normally given him some cause for concern had his animal instincts not already kicked in.

Odd little comments and actions did spark a raised eyebrow but he put that down to her youth and exuberance. And indeed, after only their third drink, Beverley stood up, picked up her handbag and casually said,

"Come on, back to mine."

A little taken aback, Ray initially thought her rising to her feet was her desire to pay a visit to the ladies and momentarily was slow off the mark.

"Well, coming or not?" she pushed for an answer.

"Yeh, sure" and quickly finishing his pint, he followed her out of the wedged open front door.

"Come on shy-boy," the man-eating vixen called over her shoulder, already two paces ahead. Ray had been called a few things in his time, but shy-boy had never been one of them.

Pausing at a soft-topped red sports car, she held the keys up and asked,

"Wanna drive?"

"No, I'm happy just to ride along." He was not ready to divulge any of his inabilities just yet.

"Not bad hey" Ray marvelled at the cream leather interior. The memory of Clarkey's wreck came flooding back, the contrast was poles apart.

"Yeh, Mum and Dad bought it for me when I passed my test last year." And turning to face the road ahead, her right foot put the pedal to the floor and in a terrifying burst of acceleration they left the public car park in a cloud of dust.

Screeching to a halt some ten minutes later at the stone cobbled forecourt of her immaculate eighteenth century farmhouse, she smiled with self-satisfaction. Walking through the unlocked heavy oak, bolt studded front door, Ray followed as a pet dog might. The date stone revealed the exact construction date of 1709 with the name 'Curzon Farm,' in bold carving above.

Kicking off her shoes, she casually nodded to the fridge and asked,

"Bubbly?"

"Yeh, why not?" Ray was almost speechless; she seemed to model herself on some actress he'd seen in some movie about the rich and famous. But what happened next, Ray had to pinch himself, "Have I just entered the twilight zone?" he whispered to himself.

Taking a large gulp of champagne, she placed her glass on the enormous pine kitchen table and proceeded to provocatively undress.

"Aren't your parents in?" He looked around as if it was possible someone lurked within the shadows.

But she mouthed a shush and put her finger to his lips in order not to spoil her routine.

"Yeh but they might come in," Ray persisted.

"They live in the other half of the house, now shush and enjoy."

And with some reservations, Ray managed to oblige.

**Chapter 25** **7th June 1977**

"Hi Mum!" Ray, feeling somewhat down approached his mother on letting himself into her lifelong council home. Giving her a kiss on the cheek, he asked,

"Is this you for the day?"

"Oh yes, there is a street party but I don't think I'll bother, it looks like rain."

The Queen's silver jubilee celebrations were underway and she was glued to the television, commemorative mug in hand.

"Beverley not with you?" she half heartedly enquired.

"No, back at the farm, busying herself," he unconvincingly informed her.

"Hmmm." Edith Taylor did not much care for her son's wife. He had made a mistake and she knew that he knew it too, but he's made his bed, so it's his to lie in or do something about it.

Ray was bamboozled at the level of railroading involved in the events leading up to the wedding. Beverley just managed to mention that Ray was 'the one' over dinner one evening with her parents, Jim and Eunice. At that point the buggy was firmly placed on the rails and gained momentum daily. His vision was one of the hand-pumped maintenance trucks that you see on westerns or silent movies, being furiously worked by Beverley's odd parents.

Odd being the operative word, it would not be totally uncommon for them to be sauntering around the house naked. Beverley thought it completely normal and would not bat an eyelid on bumping into them. Yes they have their half of the farmhouse, but only an unlocked door separates the two sides. Beverley received her part of the property on her eighteenth birthday from the liberal couple, after a lifetime of spoiling.

This is brilliant, Ray tried to convince himself, everything was to be handed over on a plate, but deep down he knew it wasn't quite right. Small comments were strategically placed in conversations; conspiracy theorists would have a field day.

'When you work on the farm' or 'You get used to the mornings eventually' would be slipped in over meals or lavish drinking parties. Ray assumed they meant helping with haymaking or occasionally mucking out the horses. But oh no, and one almighty row had broken out when the cards were laid on the table, but only done so after the wedding.

Last night's eruption saw Ray and his wife sleeping in separate rooms for the first time. Her nymphomaniac bedroom Olympics had already slowed down to a grinding halt now that he was well and truly in the bag.

"You need to pack that job in now and start work on the farm full- time," and "You can forget going out with your mates, you don't need them anymore," were like a red rag to a bull to Ray, the main emphasis being placed on the word bull. Ray felt like he had been selected, as a land owner would find one for his cows. Didn't they hold 'farmer's balls' so to speak, so likeminded people could find a mutual relationship, or had they already been scared off? Well if they think Ray Taylor will just fall into line, they are barking up the wrong tree, or more appropriately ploughing through the wrong field.

So with no son and heir to take over, just a spoiled rotten daughter and an ageing farm hand, a cynical selection of bloodstock had taken place, seemingly in order to pick up the day-to-day running of the farm. Pig shit Pete, the permanently filthy, hired labourer would soon have milked his last cow and was about to call it a day. Ray had never seen the one toothed, unshaven, weather-beaten man clean!

So tonight he would make a stance and sleep at his mother's after the jubilee party in the park. Albeit with Beverley's parting words of, 'Oh and by the way, I'm pregnant!' still rebounding around his head.

**Chapter 26** **16th June 1977**

Ray watched as the modest gathering shuffled into the small chapel. Beverley's scowl at Val and Thomas echoed a deafening silent message 'stay away from my husband!' She needn't worry herself; Val's feelings for Ray were non-existent.

If only he hadn't left his mother alone to go and selfishly try and drown his sorrows, he again agonised. 'See you later' and that was it. He would never say another word to her again, not as a living person at least. They could have spent the afternoon together and when it happened, he could then have used his first aid skills to save her. But in his heart of hearts he knew it was her time and it was meant to be.

Remembering the day in question, he had moodily watched the festivities at the celebrations and only partook in a modest amount of the badly kept beer. Not really wanting to socialise, he watched the next generation of youthful drinkers overindulge themselves. He casually watched them increase their stupidity as the alcohol in their blood increased accordingly. Their boisterous behaviour had the effect of splitting the crowd's opinion as one of them, a curly haired geeky sort, went to use the portaloo. Once he had turned the lock, the rest of the gang tipped it on its side and rolled it around a large grassed area. Then standing it back upright, they allowed their friend to exit. The sight of the poor young man drenched from head to foot in urine left the youths in hysterics, with everyone else divided. As for Ray, he would have once been the main instigator.

He also took this time in virtual solitude, trying to assess his options. He could go and live back at home, but could that be possible now his mother had gone? And continue life as though nothing had happened. His thoughts not even caring to consider the unborn child he was bitterly informed of, just yet at least. Or go back and live a restricted existence, albeit in 'luxurious surroundings,' farm graft aside. Truth is he didn't know, he still didn't, it was not going to be an easy decision. The lavish wedding, marquees and all that was just a facade, but oddities withstanding, there were no stereotypical farmers with padlocks on wallets in this family.

Closing his eyes as he recalled his return home, he was going to discuss his problems with his mother. They would surely sort it out between the two of them. He was probably missing an obvious solution. Placing his key in the lock of the, much in need of a lick of paint, front door, he found something was preventing his entrance. Pushing and shoving, the realisation that his mother's vacated shell was the resistance, totally shocked him. Fear, panic and grief were instantly rolled into one. His 999 call though, need not be rushed, so his words of apology for the person he had become to the person who had given him life, felt apt, if not a little late.

Looking up, he found his father was staring at him across the pews. That would be an added problem. No doubt he would be interested in the proceeds of his late wife's estate. But that could be dealt with at a later date. 'Where there's a will there's a squabbling family' he recalled someone saying.

And as for another saying, whether it was the correct meaning or not, 'curtains' he'd heard the gangsters say in the movies, James Cagney, New York accent and all, meant their closing at the solemn crematorium, was Edith Taylor's final bow.

**Chapter 27**

The sight of Ray being dropped off at work turned a few heads and raised some eyebrows. The red sports car screeching into the parking area of the fire station yard was far in excess of anyone's idea of safe driving. Giving his wife a peck on the cheek, as he stepped from the gleaming status-symbol, induced looks of envy from all with one exception.

The sunny morning saw his colleagues outside, taking the early lukewarm rays onboard, before their day shift began. Virtually all with cigarettes in hand came one by one to commiserate him on his loss.

"Sorry to hear about your mother Ray."

"Yeh Ray, if there's anything I can do..." another patting him on his upper arm added, and so on. Just one face quickly thought of something more important he needed to be doing at that exact moment.

"Yeh, thanks lads." There was nothing else he could add.

His brain was awash with problems awaiting solutions and the standoff he had always endured with Tony Jenkinson was just one of them he didn't need right now. What was his gripe with Ray? He didn't know, but an awkward toleration was as good as it had ever got. Today, he told himself, he would just come out with it and ask.

As for his troubles at home, for the sake of a peaceful life, he had made a compromise of learning many aspects of farm life on his days off. This along with one night out per week, but he 'would not, repeat, would not, pack in his job.'

'Ok, for now,' Beverley said, almost out of earshot. He did consider an on the spot argument, but he couldn't stomach the thought of it just then.

His father had again, for the fourth time this week been sniffing around his former home, probably for anything of value. But if he ever decides to move back in, that would be one door shut on Ray's options. 'Bloody hell, I don't need any of this shit right now' he said to himself as he stubbed out his cigarette with the ball of his foot.

Lunch out of the way; he told himself 'well if nothing else, I'm going to get to the bottom of at least one problem'.

Putting his feet up for a post-lunch forty winks Tony 'Jenko' Jenkinson was disturbed by a man on a mission.

"We've worked with each other a while, what is it, eight nine years Jenko, but we haven't really got on have we?" Ray opened his speech. "I just think it's time we settled our differences, I don't need any crap. Life's too short and all that."

"You really don't know do you?" He returned a look that if not hatred, was immense dislike.

"To be honest, no, I don't really know, tell me."

"Ok then, where do I start? You get away with murder you do. You piss around, you drop loads of bollocks, and you come to work anywhere from half cut to completely blathered and guess what? You always come up smelling of roses. So Yeh, it's safe to say I don't like you, in fact I can't be doing with you."

"Right, that's told me then." Ray tried a weak smile.

"You should have been sacked years ago, but even if you did, you'd land on your feet. Look at you; you've now almost got yourself a fuckin farm!" Jenko's blood was boiling and he was set to leave.

"I'd swap my problems for yours if that's how you're looking at it" Ray calmly spoke.

"Yeh sure, red sports car, cracking blond wife, part of the landed gentry, sure you would."

"So that's it, you're jealous."

"Like fuck I'm jealous" he bitterly retorted.

"Well why don't we try and call a truce?" Ray tried for a compromise.

"Fuck off, and if I get chance I'll drop you in it agai..." tailing off, his words gave realisation that he was the management's mole.

On several occasions, Ray along with some others, to a lesser extent, had received warnings from the offices of upper management for misdemeanours that should not have left station level, in regards of disciplinary measures.

Cursing himself for his slip up, Jenko's persona changed.

"Er, I didn't mean, ...grass, ...er tell the bosses, I wouldn't." He began to fret, "Ok then truce." There was an onset of panic.

But Ray's look of disgust left him cold, the others would now know of his sly tactics.

"Well?" he called out as Ray turned his back. He considered saying 'I ain't no grass,' but he wanted

Jenko to stew in his own selfish miserable juices, after all, Ray deserved a change of luck surely?

## Chapter 28

"Mum, you shouldn't be here." Ray found his mother wandering around his bedroom.

"Why not? I should be able to see where my son lives."

"That's not what I mean Mum." Ray found that dead people, including his mother, sometimes don't actually know they've passed on. It was also embarrassing to have to inform them of the fact.

"You know, you're, how can I say it? Gone to live with Grandma and Granddad."

"Oh yes silly of me, I forgot" and she apologetically shied gracefully away.

But Ray had got it sussed, he was dreaming. After weeks of not being able to distinguish them from reality in the room that was devoid of light, he had found a way. 'Ah ha' he would say to himself, 'I'll know if this is a dream, because I can float in my dreams' and in doing so, a peaceful-ish night's slumber could be resumed.

But this time she returned and was crying.

"Raymond, I'm scared for you." she sobbed uncontrollably.

"Mum, I'm ok, please Mum, don't cry, Mum, Mum, MUM!"

He woke in sweat, with the sheets around him soaking wet. He put his arm out to touch Dawn, only when she woke, it was unloving, unsympathetic Beverley.

"Shut up, it's just a dream," she sleepily yet still abruptly informed him.

Ray was in a state of shock and just wanted to be held and reassured, but her back was firmly and uncompassionately turned.

Stopping himself, as he was just about to switch the light on, he could hear a noise outside near the outbuildings. Ray found his heart was pounding. Had his mother somehow tried to warn him? Creeping into the darkness of the kitchen with only a slither of moonlight finding its way indoors, he could just make out the time. It was 3.15am. Surely Jim and Eunice's soiree, as they put it, had long since finished. Then he saw the briefest of movements by the barn, but it was gone in a flash. Picking up a heavy doorstop in the shape of a black Spanish bull, he, completely naked, turned the key to warily go outside to investigate.

Fuck! There was more than one of them, another was round the back of the shippen and appeared to be trying to catch up with the other perpetrator at the barn.

"Shit, I should have put some shoes on!" he cursed as a sharp stone caught his instep. But he had been heard because a third person was now fast approaching from behind. Turning quickly in order to intercept an oncoming attack, fear was replaced with a surreal state of shock. A woman, perhaps mid fifties touched his shoulder with the tip of her finger,

"Tig, you're mine"

"What the?" But he for once was lost for words, as she in turn was barring a pair of flip flops, unclothed.

"Come on, the barn is made up for fun and games."

"What? No, I'm not part of any game." Ray was still coming to grips with what was unfolding. She looked at him from head to foot.

"Course you're not darling, but if what you see is not what you want, then it's your loss." and she was off.

Investigating further, he peered through the side door of the barn. Ray had never seen the likes of it before. Well, he had but only in magazines. He was after all a man of the world. Swings, medieval stocks and various contraptions he couldn't put a name to were in position for who knows what.

A plump man was tied to one of the main pillars of the barn and was being whipped by a woman in what looked like a black leather catwoman outfit.

"Jeeesus" Ray whispered to himself, she was drawing blood with the lashes to his backside. But strangely, judging by his erection he was somehow enjoying the experience. "Fucking hell, this can't be happening!" tight lipped he gasped, as his father-in-law, clad only in a pair of riding boots wielding a horse-whip joined in the proceedings.

Creeping back inside the sanctuary of his own kitchen, he went to the drinks cabinet and poured himself a large scotch.

"Bloody hell, this would be funny if it wasn't so close to home," he muttered to himself. "Christ, I'm as broad minded as anyone," he went on, "but this, and what's more, where did all that equipment come from? It must be hidden under the bales of hay." Ray was totally aghast.

He knew Jim and Eunice were different, eccentric even, but full blown orgies and cavorting toffs, this was weird. "This happens... well I don't know where; perhaps London or Paris, but not on a farm in Northern England." Again he shook his head in disbelief.

Touching his own shoulder, he realised how cold he was and taking a last gulp, however sleepless he was, he returned to bed.

"Brrr, you're freezing, where have you been?" Beverley asked.

"Downstairs and outside, er, do you know what's going on out there?" Ray tentatively asked.

"What that lot? Yeh, each to their own," she somewhat surprisingly stated in a casual manner.

"But your Mum and Dad, don't you mind?" Ray couldn't believe that this was the norm in any family.

"They used to be more discreet when I was younger but since they split the house in two halves, they do as they please."

"Does it happen often?"

"Nah, twice, three times a year that's all, here at least."

"You mean other people hold these... these events?"

"Oh Yeh, but this is the 'big one', out of the way of prying eyes." Her matter of fact acceptance astonished him.

Ray wanted to know more but Beverley yawned and sighed,

"Can we go back to sleep now?"

"Yeh but, oh it doesn't matter." Ray's mind was racing, the whole caboodle made his head spin. Then shaking his head, he pictured a strange vision, then instantly dismissed it. 'Nah, surely pigshit Pete wasn't one of the revellers!'

## Chapter 29

"Jim, Eunice." Ray nodded his head at his wife's parents, life it seemed had returned to normal. It was as if last night's activities had not even happened. He half expected an explanation or apology, but none were forthcoming.

"More tractor lessons after lunch Ray?" Jim asked.

"Yeh... ok... about... one-ish." Ray spoke slowly, in some way trying to get in the mindset of his father-in-law, but that it seems was a totally separate entity. So tractor lessons it was. He could cope with driving it around. However, it was with all the other aspects that were still proving hard to come to terms with; a little like married life itself, he reflected.

"Ok Ray, we'll do some reversing," Jim informed him.

"Yeh, ok," Ray simply replied, he could do that given enough room.

"Right, we'll hitch up that hay-baler over there." Jim had decided that reversing without towing a piece of equipment is only useful a part of the time.

Ray could feel his blood pressure rising; he hadn't expected this obstacle in his learning. He knew this wasn't easy, he'd seen experienced drivers struggle with manoeuvres when turning.

"You ok Ray?" Jim observed Rays outward nervous signs.

"Isn't there something else needs doing?" he began to try and wangle out of the training planned for him.

"Come on Ray, you're going to have to come to terms with the machinery and moving it around."

"Yeh but Pete can do that for now and I could be on with something else" Ray tried his hand.

"Nonsense, Pete won't be here forever, you need to get to grips with it."

The baling machine safely hitched up to the tractor, Jim began "Ok Ray, let's just get used to going forward."

Surprisingly Ray found that the piece of machinery he was towing followed neatly behind.

"See, not too bad," Jim nudged Ray's shoulder with his own.

"Ok, pull up at the side of the barn." Then he began to explain the next stage.

"What I want you to do is to reverse around the side, so you are parked in front of the shippen." Again Ray began to feel tense, he knew the principle of reversing with something in tow and he knew his own limitations.

"Firstly make sure you are parked nice and straight then slowly start to reverse, then when I say so, turn the steering wheel the opposite way to normal reversing." Jim made it sound so simple.

But in doing so time and time again, Ray spectacularly got it wrong. Fearing Ray was about to lose his temper, but more so for his expensive baling machine, Jim thought of an idea. Ray was all flustered; he sensed Jim was secretly making it hard in order to poke fun at him.

"This is what I propose Ray, we'll uncouple the baler and put on that old flat backed trailer." The fact that there was no response did not deter him.

"Then we'll drive out into the top field, put some cones out and you can get used to reversing around them. No harm can be done that way." Jim felt this was best under the circumstances.

'Now he thinks I'm stupid,' Ray thought to himself, but Jim knew exactly what he was thinking.

"You can do this Ray; what I'm going to do is put the cones out, then leave you to it. You can spend as much time as you want, no one will be watching and if you need me, I'll be in my office. You'll get there in the end trust me. It's the same for everyone."

Ray had heard those words before when it came to driving, but did feel a lot happier that no eyes would be upon him to criticise.

Four hours later he was beaming with pride. Yes, his head was bouncing with tension but eight times out of ten, he could back the trailer to somewhere near where he wanted it. Unhitching the trailer in the exact spot he found it and putting the tractor in the barn, he remembered last night's shenanigans. There were absolutely no indications of what had happened. He expected to find spots of blood where the overweight man was being whipped, but nothing.

"Takes all sorts." He found he was talking to himself again. "Large scotch for me," and he happily headed off to his own and his unlikely wife's segregated life.

## Chapter 30 November 1977

'Bitch!' Ray frowned at the alarm clock, it was 9.15am. Why he expected Beverley to wake him in their separation within the segregation of their home was anybody's guess. Standing up too quickly didn't help either. Grabbing hold of the bedside drawers in the nick of time stopped him from falling over. Finding he was so lightheaded, he stood for a minute, taking deep breaths in an effort to raise the oxygen level in his blood.

His mouth felt terrible, he could still taste the whisky that was so readily available. 'That's the problem,' he muttered to himself. 'Beer doesn't make me like this, its Jim's endless supply of fine scotch.'

He also wouldn't have done what he did if it were not for the potent yet smooth spirit. 'Yeh, it was the booze that made me do it.' Still rambling on; 'She would wind the Pope up, she would.' An argument a fortnight ago ended up with his hands around Beverley's neck, only ending when Eunice came to investigate. Now he was late for work and blame needed to be put somewhere.

Stepping outside into the cold damp air, he immediately slipped. The muck spreader had flicked slurry near to the front door. That combined with a tap being left on had made conditions treacherous and pigshit Pete he decided was to blame. 'But wait a minute,' he was at it again, wittering to himself, 'that can be my excuse for being late, tell them I fell but soldiered on into work, Yeh, that'll do.' He was quite pleased with himself.

Ray shivered, he hated the prospect of another winter, that's why he packed up working on the building sites; it was also the reason his share of the farm duties had dried up, and he had no real intentions of ever starting them again. But a little happier now a plan had been formulated, he carefully weaved his way down the slippery farm track that led to the main road into town.

Jumping off the number 12 bus, he remembered just in time to limp as he entered the fire station by the rear entrance. Mind you, come to think of it, he was a bit sore. He'd banged his tailbone or coccyx. He could make a joke of that, try and make light of his situation.

"Bloody hell Ray, where have you been?" Then stepping back and waving his hand over of his face, Dave Ball exclaimed "Woh! How much have you had to drink?"

"Why is it noticeable?"

"Noticeable? I could get pissed just talking to you!"

"What have they said about me not turning in on time?" Ray tried to get some up front information.

"It's been noted, Steel and Naylor are here."

"What, for me? Surely that's a bit over the top?"

"They were coming anyway, but then they found you were AWOL."

"Shit, just my luck." Ray accepted defeat; another warning is on the cards.

"Looks like it's gonna happen." Dave thought it time to bring Ray up to speed on the unfolding events.

"What's gonna happen?" Ray had forgotten.

"The strike, seems we're going out."

"No way, everyone said it wouldn't come to that."

"I know but... shit they're here." Dave's words were cut short by Ray's arch enemies, stepping up sides.

"Ah Mr Taylor, nice of you to join us, and it does look like you did manage to organise that brewery booze up." His sarcastic icy tones sent Dave sloping off, to leave Ray alone to face the music.

"I think we need to have a good chat about your future, but for now we'll say you have taken a day's leave shall we?" But before Ray could think of a contribution to the conversation, Steel continued,

"And if you and your colleagues decide to go ahead and strike, you may all be searching for new employment before too long." The tone of his voice sounded extremely cold and threatening.

Tensions had been stretched at work for the last week or so, as hard talk headed towards hard action. Truth is most men can't afford to strike and the management knew it, so chess championship style mind games were now thrown into the cauldron.

"Ok Mr Taylor, please leave the premises, it's your day off, we'll talk again when all this nonsense is sorted. Steel decided to assert his authority in front of the rest of the men.

"Right, everyone else to the lecture room, see if we can't make you see sense, who ever heard of the fire brigade going on strike?" Naylor now assumed it was his duty to flex his managerial muscle in the impending drama.

Ray sure didn't feel like going home, not just yet at least. So in dire need of food to soak up the alcohol still in his blood, 'Dirty Shirley's' would be his next port of call.

"Hello cheeky, not seen you in here for a while" Shirley Collins the establishment proprietor fondly removed her cigarette to welcome him into the modest yet somehow homely back street cafe.

'Dirty Shirley's', actually named 'Shirl's Cafe' had been nicknamed, not because of any substandard practices within her business venture. It was down to her more youthful years as the town bike. And Ray can vouch that many a young man had taken a ride.

"You seem a bit down, what's up?" Shirley had a look of genuine concern on her face.

"Oh, this and that" Ray was in no mood to share his troubles, not here at least.

"What can I get you then? Full English and a cup of strong tea? That'll sort you out in that department, then we can have a chat later, how does that sound?"

"Yeh great Shirl, thanks." Maybe he would indulge her in some small talk after his fill.

"Blimey you were hungry, can I get you some more?" Ray was mopping up the saucy remains with a slice of bread and butter. But by holding his hand up and shaking his head, due to his mouth being full, signalled a decline for more. Finishing off with a large slurp of tea, he then slapped his belly with both hands to demonstrate fulfilment.

"What's this I hear, you got yourself married to some farmer's daughter, is it true?"

"The less said the better." Ray's guard was still up.

"That good eh?" Shirley wanted to know more but realised she would have to find another way to loosen his tongue. "Listen, I finish about two o'clock, why don't we go for a drink?"

"What, down the Con club?" The conservative club would have to suffice due to the afternoon closing of pubs.

"Yeh, why not?" He would be ready for a drink anytime soon.

"Con club it is then. I'll be there soon after two" Shirley concluded.

Picking his coat up from the back of the chair, Ray's immediate thought was, 'here we go again,' but then decided on 'at least it'll teach that stupid cow of a wife who's boss!'

He was already on his fourth pint when Shirley arrived and she had to beckon him out of the snooker room. Women not being allowed in that part of the club would have seen her drinking alone. However Ray put one finger in the air signalling one minute and judging by the pink and black only remaining on table, the game would soon be over. She could wait; good gossip was to be had, and hopefully an end to hear enforced celibacy, due to an absence of offers over the last two months.

Following a one sided, scaled down version of events Shirley got her way by means of consoling the poor innocent victim, but only after another three drinks.

Taking in his surroundings along with long draws of cigarette smoke, he reflected on the scale of this latest downturn. Replacing the luxurious splendour of his bedroom at home, this was not squalor, but a tired slightly run down, basic, room above a cafe and what's more, a bed spring was poking his arse! All this is a one-off, he told himself. He certainly would not be boasting around town of this latest conquest. Swinging his legs out of bed Shirley asked in a slightly hurt way.

"Aw, you're not off yet are you?"

"Yeh I suppose I should be" Ray now sobering up a little, didn't fancy seconds.

"Back off to wifey are you?" Now sounding a little bitter, she continued. "Thinks you've been at work all day, she would have a surprise if she knew where you've actually been."

If looks could kill, Ray's would have meant an instant execution.

"You know I wouldn't though, don't you? I was only joking." Shirley's climb down was a spectacular freefall.

"Shirley that was a shag, nothing else, and it's what we do, both of us, what do you expect?" He wanted to continue but words escaped him.

"Yeh, good old Shirley-shag-bag, that's me."

"Shirley you can be a nice person, but please don't come on all heavy, let's just take it for what is or was." His past tense correction, the confirmation that is where what happened between them belonged and would not be ongoing.

Arriving home just after eight o'clock, Ray was surprised and a little taken aback to find Jim sat at his kitchen table. A bottle of scotch and two glasses were awaiting a second recipient.

"Sit down Ray." Jim succinctly instructed him. Somewhat puzzled at this unexpected occurrence he did as he was told; resisting the urge to question the intrusion into Ray and Beverley's half of the house.

"We need to talk" He simply informed him.

"Yeh sure, go ahead." Ray was wary in his reply.

"Beverley has given birth early this afternoon; you were unavailable at the station, so you could not be made aware of the fact." Ray was quickly trying to formulate a plan, but Jim took the silence as Ray's usual uncaring self.

"Both are doing well in case you're interested."

"Oh Yeh, I was about to ask." This even sounded pathetic to Ray himself.

"Right let's get down to the nitty gritty, I have a business proposal for you." Jim was in no mood for pussyfooting around. "What I'm about to offer you is a one off, no compromises, deal." And pulling out a cheque book and pen he continued.

"£10,000 and you walk away; the baby's surname will be Curzon and you will have no say in its future. You will agree to a divorce as soon as you receive the paperwork and we will never see you again."

Ray took a minute to digest the information before simply asking, "Is that it, take the money and run?"

"Got it in one, Ray," he would have loved to say 'unlike your driving' but this was neither the time of the place.

Ray didn't see he had an option, he didn't relish the prospect of a lonely life on the farm, ostracised by his wife and now her family.

"Ok then."

"Righto! Pack your bags and be gone first thing," then signing the cheque he ripped off the slip and handed it to Ray.

"Oh and by the way, it's a boy; since you haven't even bothered to ask." Jim's look was now one of disgust at his son in law.

"Ah that's it, got your heir to the fortune now have you?" Ray now understood the whole package. He just wished he had handled their little tete-a-tete somewhat better.

"£10,000 should buy you a modest place, now do I have your assurances of sticking to the bargain?"

"Yes" Ray decided to leave the conversation with that one simple word.

"You understand Ray, that I have everyone's best interest at heart but most of all, my grandchild's," were Jim's final parting words as he turned his back to leave through the connecting door.

## Chapter 31 December 1977

"Bollocks to this, I'm off to the pub" Ray had finally reached the end of his tether.

"You can't Ray, we've got to stay and man the picket line." Len Holloway again spoke up.

"Who says so? What are the rules? We're on fucking strike, we're not getting paid, the management can't touch us and the union are just pissing about. This should all be sorted by now; and what's more it's fucking freezing."

"Ray's right. Let's take it in turns to go and get a pint or go home 'n get warm; as long as somebody stays, what difference does it make?" Barry supported Ray's logic.

"Well I'm skint, so I ain't coming. Maureen would go mad if she found out I was spending money we haven't got." Dave Ball put his own slant into the conversation.

"Right I'm buying, whose coming?" Ray couldn't imagine anyone would choose to sit by a brazier trying to keep warm in preference to the inside of the nearby White Lion. "Well?" He was waiting for someone to make a decision.

"I'm staying." Len's predictable choice was no surprise.

"Yeh! I'll come. Dave had also had enough."

So after much debate six of the twelve broke ranks to see out the last hour of drinking time in relative comfort. But the main topic of conversation, out of earshot at least, was where 'had Ray come by his seemingly endless supply of money?'

To confound his problems, he was now confronted by a standoff in the Taylor household. Ray had moved back in, but his father stubbornly refused to leave the former matrimonial home. Arguments were plentiful, mainly over the rent payments, and it was Ray who was copping for his father's share. His main dilemma was, if he paid him off, say £500 to move away, it would just be the tip of the iceberg, as he would just keep turning up for more, like the proverbial 'bad penny.'

He could of course use the fast dwindling money for its intended purpose, or at least use some as a deposit to buy a place of his own, but he was attached to the home. So for now his plan was to make life uncomfortable for Mr. Taylor senior.

Small tricks, like only buying enough food for one; or sabotaging the electrics by taking out the fuses, were some of Ray's tactics. But harebrained schemes on a grander scale were resisted; like staging a fire to send him packing or paying yobs to scare him from the vicinity.

Ray bided his time until a good idea turned up that would finally pay dividends. In the end it was just that, time or lack of it, which is the one that gets us all eventually, that caught up with Harry Taylor.

At first it was the coughing up of blood, then the slight coming and going of jaundice until his skin took on a permanent nicotine yellow pallor. All it took was six weeks from the first visible signs, to the outside world at least, to his bitter deathbed exit.

Ray felt no emotion, neither sadness nor elation at the passing of the man he had despised for so long. It was just a matter of fact, but maybe some alarm bells should now be ringing. He was conveniently ignoring the fact of the similarity of the lifestyles he and his father had enjoyed. His father was sixty-three, his mother, sixty-two. A time-bomb was well and truly ticking.

**Chapter 32** **March 1978**

"We know you're in there Ray, so just open the door and pay your dues."

The menacing voices that were making demands through his letterbox really should not be ignored, but surely if deterred long enough they would see reason. Following his father's funeral, heavies from the Tooth Fairy Loan Company have been on his case. It appears that he had run up a debt with Reg Priestley's organisation before his death and the sum owed was snowballing.

"It's not my debt, I've borrowed nothing."

"Technicalities Ray, technicalities!" He informed him that the debt was still alive, if indeed Harry Taylor wasn't. The only proof that it existed at all was in the little black book that he, or one of his oversized thug's, taunted him with by waving it in the air.

"You bastard, you're still haunting me." He cursed his father glancing upwards when surely; he should have been looking down to the other place. It was the 1st of February when it first came to light to Ray. The alleged sum owing was £800, but it now stood at a staggering £1200, so what were his options? Go to the police, pay off and be done with it, or carry on duckin and divin? Trouble is the latter at some point would entail a good hiding, as surely would option one. So his decision made, well sort of, would involve negotiation.

"Give me some proof of the original debt." Ray sat crouched by the door in reply to their demands.

"It's written down in the book Ray. Harry Taylor - £400 - November 1977, with you as a guarantor."

"Yeh, but he's dead, I've never seen a penny. He was always skint. I never saw any money." Ray offered a plea. "How do I know he ever borrowed it in the first place?"

"That's not very nice Ray. I find it very upsetting to be called a liar." Reg sounded genuinely hurt. "My boys don't like me to get upset, do you lads?"

The silence that filled the pause in proceedings, Ray imagined was taken up with his tooth extracting bully's shaking their heads.

"Ok then, I'll give you the £400." Ray opened his gambit.

"Come on Ray we know you've had some good fortune, pay up and be done with."

That was it; they have made up a debt. That was one that could neither be proved nor disproved on hearing of his payoff from Jim. Maybe, even he was in on it, he had not thought of that before, his brain was going into overdrive.

"Right, £800 and we'll call it quits." Ray upped his offer.

"Only too happy to take £800, but the remaining £400 will still be live; so it's up to you." The ungenuine joyful voice echoed into the hallway.

"Come on Reg, meet me somewhere in the middle; after all it's not my debt," he again pleaded for a bargain.

"Families eh Ray, who'd have 'em?"

"Reg, cut me some slack." Ray unrealistically thought this might get him somewhere, "That bastard even left me to pay for the funeral." 'Yeh that's it, play the sympathy card.' "Never paid his way, always left it to me to bail him out," he continued.

"Oh Ray, you poor soul, let me get my violin out." Ray had a vision of a mocking, sob story fiddle-playing Reg Priestley.

"Ok Ray what's it to be? I've had enough letterbox chat."

It was then that someone operated Ray's mouth; well that's what it felt like,

"Fuck off I'm not paying."

"Say that again Ray, for one second I thought you said you're not paying." Reg had heard perfectly, but could not believe the stupidity of the voice emitting through the wood of the door.

"I said I'm not paying; it's not my debt. I don't owe you nowt!"

Reg thought 'you silly man and your command of the English language is poor as well,' but he was not there to hand out that sort of education.

"I'm very disappointed Ray. Now it's going to get messy."

"Yeh well, that's a maybe, but I'm not paying up so fuck off!"

"Maybe?" Reg chuckled to his posse. "We don't deal in maybes do we, boys?"

Their muffled grunts of agreement could be heard from inside the house.

"One last chance, before I go and recalibrate the debt, Raymond."

"I haven't got it, you can't get blood out of a stone" Ray's heels were well and truly stubbornly dug in.

"That's true, but boy do we have fun trying," were Reg's last words before straightening his back from his position of negotiation.

Closing his eyes, he wished he had a backup plan, but in true Ray Taylor style there was an empty space where one should ideally exist.

In essence, it was all about timing and in truth the tooth fairies probably got it just about right. They left it long enough, in case Ray had reported the incident to the police; they would be fed up of checking on him by now. His accusations would look quite lame; the fact that no harm had come to him when it supposedly looked imminent.

And as for Ray himself, as the days passed his tension eased. He was pleased with himself for scuppering their ploy. 'Thought they would try their luck with a stupid scam, well I showed 'em.' To Ray life was good again.

But in reality, the ten day cooling down period was a warm up for Priestley's mob. In fact it was boiling over when Ray found them waiting for him outside 'The Queens', after a swift lunchtime session. The broken ribs (again) mainly this time across his back, due to the leather clad fists taking their persuasive action in this region, was his physical penalty, with the addition of the customary tooth loss of course.

This was followed by a one off payment of £1800 withdrawn from his bank account the same day, along with the dental bill a week later. All this saw Ray some £2000 lighter in relation to his savings.

**Chapter 33** **August 1983**

"Mr. Taylor?" The lady looked up from her clipboard with a beaming smile.

"Yeh, who's asking?" Ray was curious at the sight of the gathering at his front door.

"Hello, my name's Judith Hodgeson and I'm chair of a newly formed committee working with the estate's residents." And holding out her hand, her smile did not dwindle until Ray took her up on the offer of a handshake.

On scrutinisation of the faces before him, with the exception of that busybody, Mrs. Butterworth from number 48, he had never, to his knowledge clapped eyes on the rest.

A pause in proceedings saw them standing in silence for only a second or two that felt much longer, 'well go on then what is it? Has someone complained about something' he wondered. But again she stood deep in thought, holding her finger on the paperwork in front of her. Then without further ado she burst into her spiel.

"Mr. Taylor, we are here to lobby the residents in relation to the benefits of 'the right to buy scheme.' I take it you've heard of the government's plan to sell off council owned dwellings?"

"Yes." He found that until all the facts were placed before him, brevity in his answers would be best.

"Well, we are here to point out, just some of the positives to as many residents as possible, in the purchasing of their own homes. Did you know for a modest sum your home could be bought, ensuring you will no longer be paying 'dead money' in the form of rent?"

"And what's more," a small bald-headed man, touching his round spectacles chirped in, "Past rent, that is to say, rent you have paid over the years will be taken into account and deducted from the amount to be repaid in the form of a mortgage." The man looked extremely pleased with his contribution. "So as you can see, it's a no-brainer, as the youth of today would put it."

"Maybe to you", Ray finally decided to enter the conversation. "Who on earth would want to buy a council house? If I ever wanted to sell it."

"Oh you'd be surprised Mr. Taylor." Another younger man, with eyebrows that appeared to be as one, spoke up. "By the fact of buying the property, the resident or should I say owner would take greater interest in the property, thus raising the value of the investment." This other doorstep campaigner now grinned with self satisfaction.

Ray again surveyed the oddities before him, Mrs. Butterworth, the only one devoid of a fixed grin was taking stock of Ray's gardening skills or more relevantly, lack of them. He hated the fact that the grass had the audacity to head so relentlessly skywards. It was mostly his fault, if he took the trouble to cut it weekly, it would take around ten minutes. But oh no, not Ray, the three monthly task would take hours and end up looking like some abstract machete-hacked wilderness.

"Have you ever thought of having your garden paved Mr. Taylor?" She could no longer contain herself. "It would raise the value of your house considerably"

"Yes it would if I owned it" Ray conceded.

"There you are; another example of how to increase your investment." Mr. Monobrow's opportunist comment sounded out.

"One last point to consider Mr. Taylor, before we leave you to absorb the benefits of this right-to-buy opportunity," Ms. Hodgeson began to round up the proceedings. "The legacy of a home within a much improved area, if ever sold by yourself, would boost the value of your estate to be passed on to your children and loved ones."

Ray took the leaflets offered but resisted any more counter arguments and having shut the door he mumbled, "Loved ones, Yeh right! My kids will want for nothing, especially not some poxy council house." Then fleetingly he considered his protégé, Thomas Wilks-Lodge and as he'd only heard his name through the grapevine, James Curzon, what exactly are they doing right now? He shook his head to resist these pointless thoughts.

Of course Ray could understand the logic behind his latest visitors reasoning, but he could not imagine anyone buying a council house, should it ever be put up for resale.

"It would be a millstone round my neck," he muttered. "And if ever there comes the day I have no money, the soft touch that is the benefits system would pay up anyway." Couldn't see a bank agreeing to that should the worst come to the worst, he reasoned with himself.

Anyway, he wasn't about to waste his next windfall on such a project. Ray's sympathetic doctor was now unwittingly assisting him play the system (no, gullible was a better description rather than sympathetic.) He felt the race was well and truly on to leave the fire service on the grounds of ill health before they could sack him. So the traumatised lumbar region of his back and the alcoholism brought about by his abusive father, would hopefully secure his future with an enhanced pension. 'Thank heavens they can't see the overplayed muscle damage, or know that the alcoholism is exaggerated, and I'm certainly no alcoholic am I?' Ray scoffed at the thought.

But in the end everyone wins, he convinced himself. The fire brigade doesn't have to look for any more reasons to hand out their final warning and in my place they can take on a more manageable, or mouldable clone type they seem hell bent on employing these days.

"So no residents lobby committee! Mr. Taylor does not want to be spending his not-so-hard-earned cash on some harebrained council-house buying nonsense," he smugly uttered as he lit a much overdue cigarette.

**Chapter 34** **November 1983**

"So what is it again?" Len Holloway was trying to understand the concept.

"A strippogram," Barry informed him.

"Yeh but she won't take everything off will she? Carole's coming later, she'll go mad if there are strippers on." He was a little apprehensive of how the evening would unfold.

"Nah, just a bit of titillation, suspenders, fancy knickers and bra, that sort of thing; it's more for fun and a piss-take of Ray."

But still Len's mind had not been completely put at ease. His wife Carole would turn the telly over at the sight of a pair of boobs and worse still kick-off if she thought he had taken some enjoyment at the flash of flesh.

A good turnout at the Conservative club's function room would see Ray into early retirement at the grand old age of thirty-seven, ten days short of his thirty eighth birthday. His official leaving date would follow that date, ensuring he would have completed twenty years' service.

Greeting friends and hypocrites alike who had made the effort to see him off, Ray chatted almost triumphantly.

"What will you do with yourself?" This seemed to be the most popular question of the evening, although many of the inquisitive well-wishers had already drawn their own preconceived conclusions. The evening however would see the absence of any senior officers. To a man, they all begrudged Ray a prosperous exit from the fire service.

"The one that got away eh, Ray?" Dave Ball slapped him on the back, just as he was about to take a gulp of his beer.

"Hey Bally, what are you having?" Ray was pleased to see another good friend boosting the numbers.

"No, I'll get these, after all, you're just a poor pensioner now" Dave joked.

"Cheers mate." Ray would genuinely miss some of his colleagues.

"It'll sure be different without you Ray, not quite so… unpredictable!" Dave smiled warmly as he engaged with his friend.

"Well, I always tried to make life interesting..." Ray held his hands out in a gesture that said, what you see is what you get.

"Whether you intended to or not, you sure did just that." Dave fondly reflected.

Then picking their pints up from the bar, both men touched glasses before downing a good third of the contents.

The police were in attendance towards the end of the evening. This was initially met with some concern; surely Ray would not be arrested on this night, of all nights. But the sight of his head disappearing into the larger than life WPCs cleavage, gave rise to roars of laughter, with the exception of Carole Holloway, who promptly marched her husband off the premises.

But unknown to Ray, for a large portion of the evening, from 9.30pm onwards at least, he was being watched. His every move was scrutinised and mentally noted. Of course Ray was so absorbed in his own world, quite rightly too, it was after all an evening held in his honour, to notice the uninvited guest.

It has been joked about many times that once embarked on a drinking session, after his second pint, Ray's alcohol level would be topped up and from there onwards ensuring he was already inebriated. This was probably true, but whatever the following quantity, his condition never really appeared to deteriorate, relatively speaking that is. It was as if his body now accepted the almost permanent intruder within his bloodstream. So yes it's safe to say he was oblivious to eyes that observed him with discreet interest.

But it was the end of the evening that saw Ray reunited with an old friend.

"Bloody hell Ray what's all this? You retiring, what's the world coming to?" It was a very talkative, Blocky.

"Blocky pal, how are you? Not seen you for ages. There have been more sightings of Shergar recently." Ray joked of the still news-worthy missing racehorse.

"I'm running for councillor, next local elections seems I've got a flair for local politics, apparently people like a larger than life character." He beamed with an air of confidence that Ray had never witnessed before.

"That's fantastic," and he eyed his old friend up, 'suited and booted' to an exceptional standard.

"Man at C&A have got a good customer there," Ray inoffensively mocked his quality attire.

"Goes with the territory, I was just leaving a meeting at the party headquarters and bumped into Terry on his way home."

"Yeh, he's been here, in fact I've had a half-decent turn out." He soulfully considered how the evening had gone.

"Well listen Ray; if there's anything I can do to help, I've got a voice in places of power, if not a seat on the council." He offered his hand as if to round things up.

"Yet," Ray delivered the single word.

"Sorry, not with you?" Blocky was a little puzzled.

"Yet, but you soon will have that seat, it's as good as yours."

"Thanks mate, we go back a long way," and with that he nodded and took his leave from the fast emptying venue.

**Chapter 35** **May 1984**

"Oo, you are a cheeky young man" the elderly lady's high pitched voice echoed out at Ray.

"So can we count on your vote this Thursday?"

"Of course you can, what's your name again?"

"I'm canvassing on behalf of Steven Blockley."

"Well Steven I shall be voting for you, you're a lovely young man."

"No no," but Ray decided to leave it at that; she would probably forget anyway. "Thank you Mrs Sutcliffe, a car will pick you up on Thursday morning at 10 o'clock."

"Bye lovey," and the door closed in his face. The noisy television inside was once more her focus of attention.

Ray had been persuaded to help out his old friend in his quest for a seat on the local council. He found he was actually quite enjoying getting out and about knocking on doors and spare time he considered was definitely on his side.

It was his meeting with Blocky a week after his retirement that rekindled their friendship, in fact he was a little touched by the whole experience.

"I can't get over you going into politics." Ray sat with a drink at the White Lion opposite the prospective candidate.

"Took me a little by surprise if I'm honest! I got talking to my Dad's friend and he just came straight out with it, so here I am embarking on a career in politics."

"But why?" Ray was intrigued by Blocky's turn around.

"Because I'm just a failed secondary modern school, council-house lad?"

"No, I didn't mean that... It's just that I couldn't imagine anyone from our school going for something like this." He hoped not to offend him.

"It's ok Ray, you're quite right, I said something similar myself. Politics are what someone else does, like writers or actors; we mere mortals are just here to make up the numbers. But one day I looked at myself in the mirror and said, hang on, why should I be bound by my own self-imposed limitations. I've not been put on this earth to accept and be trapped by mediocrity, categorised as 'nothing to offer'. So I squared up to my own reflection and said no. Right then, I decided I would flex my own mental muscles and break the chains that society would have us all placed in. And do you know who was my main vocal inspiration?"

"Who?" Ray was happy to listen.

"You were Ray; you have the patter, yes mainly for the ladies, I'll grant you that, but you have always been able to look someone in the eye and get your point across. So I pretended to be like you, in private of course, and found I do have a voice."

Ray was in total shock. He had never thought of himself as an inspirational character before. He wanted to re-enter the conversation but was momentarily speechless.

"So here I am, a potential councillor. What I lack in formal education I make up for in straight talk."

"So what happens? You just tell them what they want to hear." Ray finally found some words.

"No, you don't have to; just tell 'em as it is. This is about local politics. It's totally different from government level. Virtually everyone has the same issues, crime, Bobbies on the beat, litter, dog fouling, potholes in the roads, that sort of thing. But we've also got a core of brains behind us to tap into their knowledge when needed. So that's why we are here, to make our community a better place, after all we can't put an end to the cold war, can we? Not here at least!"

"Blocky, I don't know what to say." Ray could not believe the transformation. The man before him could not previously string two words together.

"You don't have to say anything, but I found out the hard way it's no use banging your head against a brick wall if you have a problem. What you do is go and get yourself a sledgehammer, or better yet, a wrecking ball, metaphorically speaking of course, but it's usually a matter of knocking on the right doors.

So here Ray found he was hopefully doing just that, but his main hope for now was the next punter was not going to vent his or her anger towards the Thatcher government in his direction. But whatever the problem, he was in it for the duration of the election, especially as Blocky's main opponent was one Julian Wilks-Lodge!

**Chapter 36**

The deep green eyes absorbed the visual impact of the scene set before them. Eyelashes that although real, could easily be mistaken for false, moved up and downwards in an action that was almost deliberately too slow. The other sensory organs also analysed their own share of the electric atmosphere that emitted above the musty official surroundings. Preaching to the converted in their own individual camps, gave a premature sense of security amongst the mutual appreciation societies.

Finally focusing on a smartly dressed woman, perhaps late forties, she was hastily categorised as 'giddy.' The analysis was probably incorrect, but the main target of interest was the woman's intended prey.

"Hi, Angela Charlton," she held her hand out to an unsuspecting Ray.

"Ray, er, Ray Taylor." He was quite taken aback that a particularly good-looking woman was to be found in and around the mainly dowdy collection of characters.

"I've heard quite a bit about you Ray."

"You should try not to listen to gossip; I wouldn't want it to taint your first impression."

"Believe me, my first impression is favourable, and Steven holds you in the highest regard." The woman's gaze held his eye with an air of confidence.

In an effort to fathom out the previously unheard of Angela Charlton, Ray was first to back down in the eye to eye contact encounter.

"I have it on good authority the seat's ours," she continued.

"Ours?" Ray questioned.

"Stevens, but for the party as a whole," she corrected herself.

"I hope so." Ray was not quite as confident as the pretty... no pretty was not right for Angela, her features were too severe, not unlike the images of the goddess Athena he'd once seen in a Greek restaurant.

"Look at the Wilks-Lodges, not quite so cocky now are they?" Angela nodded across the room to the main opponent protagonists.

"I think you're right." Ray silently considered he had to get a grip of himself. This woman was running rings around him, in effect, bossing the conversation.

"Why have we not met before?" Ray asked, straightening his back a little.

"Only got back from New York on Monday! Tuesday, Wednesday and today I spent on the Parkside of the ward canvassing; seems we weren't destined to meet until now." Still her eyes reached deep into Ray's.

"Why New York, was it business or pleasure?" Ray accentuated the latter with a slight twinkle in his eye, 'this was better' he told himself.

"Business I'm afraid, we hold some uneasy shares in a large engineering company and needed some face-to-face guarantees of their future."

"And did you get any satisfaction?" again almost turning the emphasis into a double entendre.

"A little, but more wouldn't have gone amiss." She now was on board with the not so subtle flirting. But that would have to be put on hold for now, as the room was descending into silence. The result was imminent with the candidates forming a disorderly line on the town hall stage.

The green eyes watched not the main event, but that of a side show involving a kind of primitive mating ritual. A lowly turnout was to blame for the Wilks-Lodges losing by forty seven votes and a re-count would be insisted upon. But the celebrations from the Blockley camp were nothing if not a little interesting. The group hug saw a firm female hand clasp the right buttock of the watcher's main focus of attention.

"Fuck me, winning doesn't half make me horny," Angela whispered into Ray's ear. He needed no interpretation of the forthright manner in which her words were delivered, but he did need to know the whereabouts of the woman's other half, most likely her husband.

"What about..." Ray tentatively enquired.

"Neville? Still in New York, and what I need right now is a good old rogering. Now where do I start looking Ray?"

No words left his lips, but his tried and tested 'get it here' look, told her all she needed to know.

"My place in an hour," she whispered then quickly scribbled the address on a piece of party-headed notepaper before heading off to congratulate Stephen.

As the observer exited the room that was now descending into anti-climax, the main post-election analysis was that of how Ray Taylor had managed to totally blank out all or mostly at least, any engagement between his own party cronies and that of the Wilks-Lodges. Had he not done so, a different outcome might have ensued, non-politically speaking that is.

"Everyone, everyone!" Blocky or more correctly Councillor Steven Blockley caught his friends and followers attention. "I don't know where to begin to thank you. I am almost speechless with gratitude to you all."

"Well don't let that continue, we need your voice," the prim Mavis Davidson called back.

"I assure you it is only temporary Mavis, and all of our concerns along with that of the constituents will be heard and more importantly acted upon." His warmth and sincerity reached all before him.

His final handshake of the long day was with that of his old friend.

"Thanks Ray, I think I can accredit at least forty seven votes to your input. You're good with people, stick around won't you?"

"Yes, I think I will," and with that, the handshake turned into a warm embrace.

"Let's all meet up for dinner, 'Napoli' perhaps?" Peter Frain suggested.

"Sounds good, 8 o'clock tomorrow ok for all?" Steven enquired. Nods from all indicated a celebration meal would be welcome at the local Italian restaurant.

And with that final note, the weary faithfully reluctantly went their separate ways.

Ray was met at the front door of Angela's large fifties built detached home with a matter of fact attitude. Opening the door, clad only in a white towelling robe bearing the name of a suave New York hotel, it gaped open revealing a glimpse of her toned tanned curves, awaiting his discovery.

"Hi, shower's running, hop in then we can get this show underway."

Doing as instructed, Ray began to formulate a list of questions as to how this presumed affair would unfold. He needn't have bothered the pristine immaculate decor would be the first indication of how Angela would prefer or rather dictate the proceedings.

Strolling into the spacious bedroom, devoted almost entirely to the colour white, he finished towelling his hair before dropping the offending item on to the heavy shag-piled floor. Painfully ignoring the misdemeanour this once, she patted the empty space besides her as if to summons his presence immediately.

The large vibrator that was neatly placed on her bedside table gave Ray his cue to try and lighten the mood.

"I don't think I can compete with that no-nonsense guy there."

"Don't worry, I prefer the real thing, but I do insist on things my way." Then with a small sigh she continued, "Ok, I would have made an exception and explained my terms afterwards, but you might as well have them up front."

Curious as to this strange pattern of behaviour, he gave a look to signal her to continue her preamble.

"We always shower first, it's a must, it's not negotiable, afterwards is up to you. It's just sex, no comforting or reassurances afterwards are needed. I would rather you leave soon after our needs are fulfilled anyhow. You don't turn up unannounced and you use discretion when coming and going. I am after all a married woman. Other than that, it's no-holds-barred lust. So if you're still up for it, let's see what you've got in your locker."

There would once have been a time when he would have left her alone with her plastic playmate and exited following a two-finger salute, but it had been a while and this arrangement might even suit. So embarking on what felt like a scrutinised examination of his skills, Ray stoically fulfilled his manly duties.

**Chapter 37**

'Napoli' was buzzing as Ray slid in at the table amongst his newfound friends.

"Thought you weren't coming, we were just about to order." Peter Frain, for all intents and purposes, Steven's understudy and main advisor, spoke up.

"Had a little errand to do, took a little longer than expected," Ray lied, suddenly not quite sure of his place within the post-election political circle.

"Ah well, you're here now," Angela chipped in without making eye contact. Discretion and mind games it seemed would be the order of the day, where she was concerned at least.

Beaming from ear to ear a friendly waiter, who may or may not have ever stood on the shores of Italy, uncorked a bottle of champagne and proceeded to share it sparingly between the eight flutes placed on a silver plated tray. Then skilfully without spilling a drop, the shiny salver was whisked around the party in order for the seated guests to take one each.

"No speeches tonight." Steven raised his glass. "Just a toast to the future," and with that, everyone dutifully repeated, "The future!"

Still avoiding any further acknowledgement, Ray decided to throw a challenge out to Angela and by taking out a cigarette; he proceeded to light up with smug satisfaction in direct opposition to last night's hissy fit. His natural conclusion to his exertions was to stereotypically indulge himself in his craving for tobacco. But this only had the effect of turning the air blue. How could he have the audacity to do so in her home? Of course he should have known better than to attempt to desecrate the sterile surroundings with his nicotine fix, but it wasn't in the rules was it? 'So Angela, are we fuck buddies or not?' Ray's eyes reached out with the unspoken question. As she looked in his direction to engage contact for what was a second longer than she would have wished, the simple answer came in the form of a stocking-clad foot in his crotch. This happened at the end of the evening when it was probable that everyone was too drunk to notice, Mavis excepting of course. But her multi-task flirting could only be admired, as she was actually simultaneously engaging Steven with some kind of seductive whispering.

Ray assumed with all probability that he was not her only lover, maybe she is a party groupie, he mused, and what of her husband? Not that it mattered, but is he stupid? Or is it a mutual open marriage? The photograph on the hallway table was that of an older man, perhaps he is just past it. All would be revealed one day, he was sure. Brought back from his trance-like daydream, Mavis was conversing with the woman in question.

"When is Neville back from America?" Her tone was one that appeared to know all too well of her marriage vow indiscretions.

"He won't be back until Sunday afternoon," was her 'none of your business' reply, but delivered so subtly; one could have easily missed it. But it was the reactions around the table that caught Ray's attention. Mavis immediately glanced in Steven's direction, Steven in Peter's, and Peter across to Ray. So he was lover number three at least, with her plastic bedside buddy filling in any gaps in her over friendly social calendar.

*So you are home alone tonight are you Angela? But who, if any of us, will get the nod?* The answer to that particular conundrum turned out to be none of the prime candidates, from the present line up at least. In all probability she got wind of the conversation that took place in the gents between Ray and Steven.

"Might be none of my business, but is there any history between you and Angela?" Ray decided to come straight out with it.

"Yes and no, I think she once would have indulged in a full blown affair had I not nipped it in the bud. Why do you ask? Has she hit upon you too?"

"You could say that. Last night I was treated to her regimental style passion."

"Yes, I've heard about her little intricacies" Steven casually stated.

"Only heard?" Ray presumed there would be more.

"At a party conference last year, Mavis caught Angela leaving my room at the hotel and I assume put two and two together to equal 'affair'.

"And there wasn't?"

"No, she wanted to ditch Peter with me as her replacement, boring she called him, too predictable. Attractive as she is, I didn't need a complication of that nature."

Ray was having a little trouble believing a hot wanton woman sneaking into his room could be snubbed.

"So nothing happened?"

"Nothing. I was sorely tempted, and it took all my willpower, but no, absolutely nothing."

"So what of Peter? Is he still in the frame?"

"I don't think so, but you never can tell with those two, the flirting will pop up sporadically."

"She looked to be whispering some sweet nothings into your ear earlier." Ray spoke of his earlier observation.

"Exactly Ray, nothings; it was probably for your benefit. She plays those sorts of games and will do so with other men if she wants to send you some kind of message."

"Message?"

"Yeh, try and make you jealous or envious; she's a complicated woman and likes things her way, always! But whatever you do, you won't be stepping on my toes, but Peter might see things a little differently." There was a subtle warning tone to his voice.

Peter, he was sure he could handle, but there was one last question,

"What does her husband make of it all?"

"They live together, but as she puts it, it's more like a brother and sister relationship and if what she tells me is true, there's no sexual involvement anymore, as they sleep in separate rooms.

"Thanks pal, I appreciate the info." Ray warmly smiled at his friend.

"Like I said Ray, it's no skin off my nose, but Peter's a different matter. He got too involved and was ready to leave his wife, so be careful."

Ray nodded in acknowledgement as the pair left the gents, only to see Angela leaving in what looked like an angry strop. Then observing the close proximity of the ladies and gents facilities, Ray could only deduct she had eavesdropped their conversation.

'Ah well, such is life,' he silently reflected, but it would be a shame if it was all over before it really began. He quite liked the idea of the dominant woman.

**Chapter 38** **August 1984**

The crash of the window breaking downstairs only had the effect of making Ray's eyes roll.

"This is getting out of hand; the police will have to get involved now." This latest, in the catalogue of 'mishaps' that had befallen Angela, or rather, her possessions, would need sterner actions.

"It's Peter; I know it is. What part of 'it's over' does he not understand?" Angela reached for her dressing gown to go to assess the damage.

"I thought Steven had had a quiet word?"

"He has, but he's denied all knowledge, says he has no interest in what was once a brief fling."

"But it was more than that wasn't it?" Ray, not the least bit jealous, just wanted to understand that part of her history.

"It was a casual on-off affair, I've told you. If Peter thought it was more, then that's his problem." Angela curtly spoke as she left the room. The matter was not up for further discussion it seemed.

So that was the deep scratch on the Audi, along with the strange spluttering of the engine. After much investigation that turned out to be a potato stuffed in the exhaust, having the effect of causing a breakdown on the motorway; not to mention the garden shed fire and the anonymous letter to Neville about Ray and some of his past indiscretions.

Maybe he should end it, he considered. Yeh, its hot sex but is it all worth it? After all, she has to live with the consequences when he has taken his leave; post-coital fulfilment.

"It's the kitchen window. Can you give me a hand to clean it up?" Angela shouted from the bottom of the stairs.

"Down in a minute" Ray called out, he was almost dressed anyway.

"Bastard, what am I going to do?" She was searching the under stairs cupboard for a dustpan and brush.

"Maybe we should publicly call it off for a while?" Ray suggested.

"It's not publicly on! This is an affair remember. Neville's family would go mad if they knew. Besides we are only assuming its Peter and the problem is 'us' that's got to him." Angela straightened up from her crouched position, cleaning equipment in hand.

"Could be kids," Ray unconvincingly offered.

"Or someone else with a grudge. Neville is quite successful and may have trodden on some toes." Angela equally unconvincingly spoke up.

"So what next then?" Ray was struggling to come up with anything constructive.

"Someone I know owes me a favour, I think it's time I called it in," was Angela's vague answer that there might be a solution to the problem.

Hitching himself up on a stool at the end of the bar in the White Lion, Ray found he had a bonus hour to kill due to his not so secret liaison being cut short. Someone was definitely a little disgruntled that his passionate meetings with Angela were still ongoing.

"Pint Ray?" Cyril the red faced, bloated landlord enquired.

"Yeh and a whisky chaser." Ray sounded somewhat deflated.

"Problem Ray?" Cyril was up for gossip on what was a quiet Thursday.

"Yeh, no, not really, not mine anyway," was Ray's unhelpful reply. But Cyril knew how to loosen his tongue.

"I've got a bottle of that Highland Malt that you've developed a liking for, if you want to pay the extra?"

"Yeh, why not, get one yourself" Ray almost absent-mindedly added.

"Don't mind if I do, thank you Ray" Cyril beamed, and then adding his own news he continued, "Oh have you heard Reg Priestley is poorly?"

"Nothing trivial I hope," Ray unsympathetically stated.

"Brain tumour, is the unofficial word, but it doesn't sound good."

"Couldn't happen to a nicer bloke," still Ray could find no absolution for the heavy handed loan shark.

"Say what you will, but you knew where you were with Reg; not like some of these modern day drug pushers. Slit your throat for fifty pence they will." Cyril spoke almost fondly of the old fashioned villain.

"Oh yes, very gentlemanly as his henchmen pummelled your midriff and broke your teeth, our Reg was, or still is, assuming he's still drawing breath."

Cyril decided to leave it there. He knew Ray had had dealings with Reg and no love was lost.

"I'm going to throw the bolt. Do you fancy sharing the cost of that bottle?" Cyril nodded to the front door, indicating calling it a night.

"Why not?" Ray looked round at the empty pub. He had nothing to get up for, and even when he did it didn't stop him, so yes why not?

"Great stuff" Cyril chuckled to himself as he secured the premises. Ray would soon be spilling out his troubles like a patient to his therapist.

**Chapter 39**

Although he had committed no crime, or none of any significance, Ray had always been nervous around the presence of the police. Even the fact that this officer was now ex did little to remove any tension.

"This is what I suggest Ange. You both just go about your normal business and I will take up a position in the woods behind your house and see if our visitor returns." Former detective Sergeant Alan Platt raised his eyebrow a little too familiarly as he emphasised the word 'business.' Ray was sure there was more to their past than the help she had given him with his application for planning permission. He consciously made a decision to find out what had actually transpired. 'Shit' was happening. Was he becoming jealous? You can't become emotionally involved in what is just sex; he re-evaluated his situation in the matter.

"If it does turn out to be Peter Frain, how do you want it to unfold?" Alan questioned.

"I don't want him arrested, is it possible to scare him off in some way?" Angela hoped for an amicable solution.

"I could make him believe he is being chased by the police and let him 'manage' to escape? He would not try to pursue this vendetta knowing he had been rumbled."

"That sounds good, he'd be thankful to get away unscathed." Angela was satisfied with the plan.

"Ok then, I'll be in place at nightfall and let's hope for a swift conclusion." Alan opened his door to let his guests out.

"Meet me at my place," were his words upon agreeing to help. "Might give the perpetrator a clue we're on to him if I turn up at yours and he recognises me, Bye Ange, Bye Ray."

Ray was sure there was a smirk on his face that said, 'been there done that.' He could not stand the fact that anyone for any reason might extract some amusement at his expense.

"Go about your business. He makes it sound like we're some kind of wild animals, my god. I'll feel like a sea lion performing on demand." Ray finally spoke of the meeting.

"I'm sure you'll manage, maybe we could have a fish supper after it if you wish?" Angela's straight face turned into a wicked smile. Then loosening up a little, he gave her a peck on the cheek before going their separate ways; Angela in her bright red Audi, Ray pub-bound, on Shanks's pony.

It was testament to his professionalism in the face of adversity that Ray managed to carry out his duties. Either that or he just plain forgot a side show was taking place around the grounds of Angela's home. In all probability it was the latter as the loud splitting of the wooden fence panel startled him so much. It catapulted him backwards from his hound-dog position.

"Jeees!" Stumbling backwards from the bed, his motion only stopped when he collided with Angela's sparkling full length mirror wardrobe, leaving a moist buttock impression on the otherwise spotless surface.

"Bloody hell Ray, what's got into you?" Angela couldn't believe Ray was so spooked by the plan coming to fruition. Reaching for Angela's dressing gown, he quickly slipped it on, despite the fact it was much too small. Pulling tight across his back and shoulders and revealing half his forearms, he was off to catch the would-be intruder. Opening the sliding patio doors he could hear Alan's voice in the distance.

"Stop, police!" Then relaxing a little, he felt a little foolish.

"Just adding to the reality," he shouted upstairs, trying to hide his impetuous behaviour. "Thought it might look better, the fact that we hadn't planned it at all." Ray continued his cover up.

"Hmmm!" Angela wasn't convinced, but a knock at the back door ended the facade.

"Only me!" Alan was shouting through the open entrance.

"Come in, I'll put the kettle on," Angela shouted down as she finished dressing.

"Well, was it Peter?" She impatiently asked, handing over a hot mug of coffee.

"I think so, fits the description and if what I'm told is correct, then yes it is Peter Frain."

"What do you mean, what you're told?" Ray entered the kitchen and the conversation.

"Well a strange thing occurred out there as I took up my surveillance position in the trees."

"Go on," Angela wanted answers.

"As I was getting myself comfortable, in good time for the onset of darkness, as my eyes became accustomed to twilight, I discovered I was not alone in watching the house."

"Go on," This time Angela and Ray spoke in unison.

"Not ten yards away, someone else was also lying in wait for Peter to arrive."

"And?" Ray was now getting impatient.

"And, I made a lunge for him, restrained and cuffed him, he's in the car." Alan nodded towards the front of the house to indicate its whereabouts.

"This was all before Peter arrived, is that right?" Angela enquired.

"Yes, I've let him escape as arranged. I don't have the powers of arrest anymore, I've just blagged this other guy. He thinks I'm undercover, so it's your call how you deal with it." Now Alan was a little unsure how to continue.

"Do we know him?" Angela spoke up.

"Maybe yes, five foot ten, dark hair, late teens, early twenties, green eyes, almost effeminate looking." Alan's voice tailed off at the end of his description of the captive. "So Ray, you better deal with it," Alan added.

"Me? Why me?" Ray was puzzled.

"Said he was looking out for you, Ray. Said he was onto Peter Frain. He's been watching him for weeks."

Ray's mouth opened but could not find exactly what to say.

"That's not all" Alan waited for effect, "There's one other thing."

"What is it?" Angela was bursting for the conclusion.

"He says he's your son, Ray." Alan delivered it with dramatic effect. "Says he was just trying to help his Dad."

The resemblance was amazing, Angela marvelled at the sight of father and son sat opposite each other at her kitchen table. The only difference was that one of them would only be breaking the hearts of other men. The fact that Ray couldn't, or more likely didn't want to see it, was one possible reason for not acknowledging Thomas's presence at various venues.

"I saw you at the council elections didn't I?" Angela softly tried to coax him into opening up. But his eyes just pierced so deeply into hers, she felt too unnerved to be dominant in any questioning. There was a short deafening silence before Angela composed herself.

"Well, are you two going to speak to each other?"

But Ray just stared at his son; yes he knew it was Thomas, the young boy he walked away from was now a man., but to what end? 'I mean, I'm not homophobic' he said to himself 'but I don't even know where to start.'

"I've been watching you for a while. I wanted to find out who I am. My parents don't know I'm here; I mean my Mum and stepfather, if you're worried they sent me." Thomas broke his silence.

"No, I didn't think they had." Ray now found some words.

"So I started secretly to follow you, just to discover who my real father is, nothing sinister. Then I found I wasn't the only one with an interest in your movements."

"Peter Frain?" Angela re-entered the conversation.

"Yes, Peter Frain. I know who he is from some of my Dad, or rather my stepfather's dealings."

"So curiosity got the better of you?" Ray questioned.

"Yes you could say that, but it was something Mum had said that I wasn't supposed to hear that intrigued me most." Thomas looked up to hold Ray's eye. "She said you have another son, a half brother to me, his name is James Curzon, is that right?"

Angela's jaw was now open, but it was Ray whose expression could not be defined. Was it shock that his past had resurfaced with such a bang, or guilt that he had made no effort to contact his sons? Most likely a combination of both, but more to his shame was that he had never even seen the face of his and Beverley's child.

"Yes," Ray finally admitted, but what could he say? He was paid off to have no part in his life. That was something that when faced with the fact, was impossible to justify to others.

"I want to meet him, can you arrange it?" Thomas coldly asked.

"I can tell you where he lives, if that's any help, but that's all." Ray decided to make it all sound a little mysterious, without making himself look like a complete bastard. And with that he wrote the address of the farm on a slip of paper. "But Thomas, be careful, they are not straight-forward people". This is more like it he told himself; lay some blame their way.

"Not straight forward, what does that mean?"

"It's not for me to blacken their name, so I'll leave you to make up your own mind." Oh yes, he was now coming into his own, being economical with the truth.

"Am I in trouble with the police?" Thomas, thankfully for Ray changed the subject.

"No," Angela answered, "The officer has left us to deal with the disturbance." She also now played her part in the theatrics.

"Thanks, Mum and Dad would be mortified if I got caught up in anything illegal."

"No one needs to know anything of what's happened here tonight." Angela put his mind at rest.

"I must go then, it's late" Thomas meekly stood from the table.

"Ray" Angela nodded across to Thomas.

"Oh yes, bye Thomas." Truth is, he just didn't know how to proceed with this father and son reunion. Thomas looked like he wanted to embrace his father, but thought better of it, perhaps it's too soon he foolishly considered. Then closing the door behind him, Angela turned to Ray,

"I think we have some talking to do, don't you?"

**Chapter 40** **July 1987**

Cyril appeared to be studying the daily tabloid intently as Ray took up his usual position at the bar. This was his tried and tested method of engaging his early doors customers into the debate of a current hot topic. In doing so it would hopefully keep them in his establishment, thus drinking for longer, in close proximity.

"I see the channel tunnel has been given the go ahead." Cyril threw out his first carrot to see if anyone would bite.

"Bloody hell, what do we want to link up with the frogs for?" Jack Haworth, an old soldier could see no benefit from an umbilical connection to Europe.

"How is it going to work? I mean, will you just be able to drive through?" Ron Kershaw joined in.

"I've heard it's going to be a rail link only." Dennis Matthews, usually the fount of all knowledge was not to be left out.

"Nah, it will be like the M6; thousands will be coming through every day." Ron was sure.

"Eh listen to this," Cyril was ready to light the touch paper of another subject. "One person is dying from aids in Britain every day."

"That's nature's way of dealing with unnatural goings on." Another punter was not going to sit on the sidelines on this hot potato.

Cyril grinned as he turned to clean some pint glasses with a towel, old fashioned style.

"Bloody hell," Jack seemed to begin all his sentences this way. "They'll be driving through to use all our hospitals; you won't be able to move, there'll be so many people over here."

"What do you say Ray?" Dennis asked the usually vocal drinker.

"Oh Yeh, we should stop it now." But his vacant expression suggested he didn't really want to make any contributions on the subjects, besides it could be a comment on either topic, so he left it there.

Ray couldn't care less about the tunnel, but the question of Aids was frequently on his mind, since his meeting with Thomas. Not that there was much contact, in fact they had only met twice since their encounter at Angela's. He could not come to terms with the fact that his son was gay. Was it his fault for letting him be brought up in what was probably a namby-pamby family? Would James also turn out this way? Could he ever be seen in the company of homosexuals? He took a large gulp of his beer as if to rid his brain of uncomfortable thoughts.

"Did you hear that Ray?" Cyril nudged him. Ray was aware of laughter around the pub.

"No, what?" Were they poking fun at him? Did they know?

"That joke Ron just come up with?"

"No, I was miles away." He hadn't heard a thing.

"Two queer cowboys, y'up, y'ip." Do you get it?"

"Oh Yeh, I've heard it before" Ray simply stated before scanning the faces around him for clues to see if they had any knowledge of his quandary.

"How this government has got in again I'll never know." Ray could hear Cyril throwing in another angle to the debate. But he had fallen out of love with his brief 'toe-dip' in the waters of politics; maybe it would be rekindled at the next general election, when Steven might step up to stand for parliament. But for now it bored him. He actually fell asleep at the party conference he attended with Angela last year.

However, he still, after three years looked forward to their Thursday trysts and following his meeting with Neville all was now above board. He was invited over one Sunday evening for drinks, which Ray assumed would be with just Angela, but his doorstep greeting from Neville almost had him back treading.

"Come in Ray, I've heard a lot about you."

On his guard and ready to scarper at a moment's notice, he did as he was instructed.

"Scotch?" Neville held a crystal decanter in order to show what was on offer.

"Yes," was Ray's slightly muted reply.

"Let's have a small chat, and then we can relax and have dinner."

Ray's mind was racing. Was this going to be an amicable 'now piss off and leave my wife alone' or an unwelcome 'ménage-a-trois' with too much testosterone in the equation?

"Cheers Ray," Neville held up his glass.

"Cheers." The talking for now would be one way.

"You and Angela; I'm here to give you my blessing. You see, sex isn't for me and to deny her pleasure of that nature would be totally unfair. Of course I've tried to, but I don't derive any enjoyment from going through the motions. Everything else, to my knowledge, is pretty good within the marriage, so I am happy for you to continue your arrangement with my wife. For my part, I will be out of town on your Thursday evening meetings and trust you will continue with a certain amount of discretion on your part?"

"Yes, discretion is my middle name," Ray thought was a fitting conclusion to the agreement.

"Great, now let's go through to see what the good woman has prepared for dinner."

Thinking back how his discomfort had turned to relaxation in Neville's company made Ray smile to himself as he sat at the bar. Hell, he even liked the man but did feel a little sorry that he couldn't enjoy sex with his wife.

"Pint Ray?" Cyril asked. "You were away with the fairies."

"Oh Yeh, whisky chaser to go with it." Ray re-focused around him. The fierce debate he would not be joining was well underway.

But he was already looking forward to tomorrow night. But how long would it continue? Angela was a good ten years older than he; would her sex drive disappear one day with the change? Or would he himself call it a day when she reached sixty? He sure would have no 'street-cred,' as the teenagers put it seeing to the needs of a pensioner, would he?

**Chapter 41** **December 1991**

Ray decided to give the pub a miss; he felt a little rough, no rough was an understatement. When he woke that morning his bed was soaking wet, fever had drained him. But what was more concerning, he felt like someone had been sat on his chest. 'It's the fags,' he told himself, 'they'll be the death of me.' Lying down on the sofa he covered himself with a blanket; his fever had turned to a chill. Turning from his side to his back felt a bit better but his chest was crackling and he was having trouble breathing.

'This is it, I'm dying.' He in no way felt sorry for himself; he truly believed it. His chill again was transformed to fever, so he closed his eyes to wait for the end.

The three small boys at his bedside were not unlike angels, all looked to be the same age, about four years old,

"Thomas?" He recognised Thomas.

"Yes, it's me, Dad."

The second child was... he didn't know his name but he recognised him, it was Dawn's son, the small downs boy he had seen in the street where she lived.

"Hello," he said, "are you going to die?"

"I think I might yes, I think I'm dying," although when he spoke he could feel no pain.

"James wants to speak to you," Thomas and the third boy knelt beside him.

"Why don't you love me dad? I'm your son." James was in tears.

"I'm sorry, I'm sorry." Ray truly was upset at the sight of his son that he had never clapped eyes on before, crying. But in an instant they were gone. A coughing fit had woken him, he had been dreaming but it was so real, he wanted to return so he could give his reassurances he would reform his character. But if this was ever going to be a reality, he knew he had to act and act fast. Crawling to the hallway he reached up to unlock the door before picking up the pale green trim phone to dial 999.

Ray was knocking at his own front door, but the strange thing was the sound was from somewhere else. He wanted to push the door open, but his mother was laid on the other side. Again the knocking started but this time he knew it wasn't him that was making the noise. He was at the dentist, that's it! He had awakened from the dreaded 'gas' following a tooth extraction. But no wait, he hadn't been back there since he was a child, but 'this was similar' he told himself. Knock, knock, click, click, the room was coming into focus. How did he get here? He slowly realised he was in hospital. A doctor was reading his notes with a pen in his mouth, clicking it against his teeth.

"Ah Mr. Taylor, good to have you back amongst us."

Ray tried to talk but his mouth was dry and something was covering it.

"Just a moment." The doctor came to his side and took off what he now recognised was an oxygen mask.

"How long have I been here?" Ray had lost all concept of time.

"Almost a week, you have been quite poorly, pneumonia" the doctor casually stated.

Then closing his eyes he drifted back to sleep.

Ray could feel someone fussing around his bed but was tired and didn't want to open his eyes.

"You awake Mr. Taylor?" A soft feminine voice skirted around the fringes of his consciousness.

"Hmm, can I have some water?" Ray sleepily replied. And with that request he could hear the noise of liquid being poured.

"Just try to sip a little, so you don't spill." The easy-on-the-ear tones reached out to him. Then opening his eyes he focused on the plump yet pretty young nurse.

"How are you feeling?" she sympathetically enquired.

"Like shi... terrible." Ray corrected his potential vulgarity.

Taking a sip of his water made him quite dizzy with exhaustion, but understanding his weakness, Lucy took his glass from him.

"Mr. Taylor?"

"It's Ray, please call me Ray."

"Ray, we have no one down on your records as next of kin, is there anyone we can notify?" Lucy found it strange that not one single person had visited him, causing much speculation amongst the staff. He was after all not an unattractive man, for an older guy at least, so why no family or friends?

"No, no one." Ray couldn't think of anyone who could be considered as next of kin. Thomas or James? Not really, no parents, brothers or sisters, he couldn't really put Angela down could he? Ray well and truly felt alone. "Just leave it blank." Now he was feeling sorry for himself.

"Ok, if you think of anyone we could contact, give me or one of the admin staff a shout." Lucy sensed there was hurt in his words.

Ray's eyes were stinging. 'It was a good time to drift back to sleep,' he told himself.

Once again Ray was aware of voices around his bed, but this time one was familiar.

"I asked him yesterday and he said he had no one as next of kin."

"Put me down as a contact, he's a good friend, no we're best friends."

Lucy seemed to recognise the well dressed man before her, but couldn't quite place him. 'It'll come to me, have I seen him on the television?' she asked herself. He really does have a presence; her old fashioned Nan would swear she was 'swooning' for the good looking man.

"Can I take your name?" Lucy realised this was probably the simplest way to solve the dilemma; she really must get her act together.

"Steven Blockley. If it makes the paperwork more straight forward, put me down as cousin."

It took Lucy a second or two to put the name to the face and if she was honest, was a little disappointed that he was only the local councillor. 'Ah well, he is surely destined for greater things,' she secretly hoped.

"Thought I recognised those silky tones, you smooth bastard!" Ray fondly spoke, without quite opening his eyes.

"Ray pal, how the hell are you?"

"I've been better, hope you're not chatting up my sexy nurse?" Ray smacked his dry tongue against the roof of his mouth.

"Here have a drink of water." Steven reached for the plastic jug and cup.

"Er, I'll leave you two to it." Lucy found she was hovering.

"How did you find me?" Ray coming round a little, was curious.

"Made me laugh, but have you ever heard of the old cliché, if you're ever missing long enough, a search party would be sent from the pub? Well I'm here!"

"Took your bloody time didn't you?" Ray joked.

"I called in for a swift one at the White Lion and Cyril was concerned that neither he nor anyone had seen hide or hair of you for days. So I called round at your place and that nosey neighbour of yours, Mrs. Butterworth is it?" Steven floated the question Ray's way.

"Yeh, that's her." Ray rolled his eyes back.

"Well Mrs. Butterworth said you were taken away in an ambulance, so I made a few enquiries at admissions and here I am, cousin Blocky to the rescue."

Ray felt moved. 'You can pack that in right now,' he said to himself. His eyes were moistening.

"You ok, Ray?" Steven had never seen his friend in any way emotional.

"Yeh, got some sleep in my eyes," and he proceeded to remove some imaginary flakiness that he had always known to be described that way.

"Is it ok if Angela visits you this evening?" Steven quickly changed the subject.

"I don't really want her to see me this way."

"Give over you vain bugger!" Steven mocked his friend's false modesty.

"Ok then, maybe I could tidy myself up a little."

"That's more like it. Now get yourself better, I'm going to need you for my up-and-coming campaign."

"So you're going for it are you? Steven Blockley MP, now that's got a good ring to it."

"That's more like it, that's what's needed in my game." Ray could see the first signs of self-doubt. He had not seen that since their teenage years.

"You'll walk it," Ray assured him. "And what's more, you've got the best back up team, so as I once said before, it's as good as in the bag."

Steven held his friend's eye and to be honest, looked as poorly as anyone he had ever seen, he sure hoped he would be there for it.

"Thanks mate," and if I remember correctly, that was my reply. But Ray's eyes were closed. He hoped he had not exhausted him.

"Is he ok?" Steven was a little anxious as Lucy returned.

"Yes, but he's very weak. It will take some time to get his strength back to normal, but yes, he'll be fine."

"That's good, he's a very good friend, please look after him."

"Consider it done, will you be back?" Lucy quickly realised she may have overstepped the mark. "I mean shall I tell him you'll be visiting again, when he wakes?"

"Yes I'll be back tomorrow." He recognised a climb down from an obvious flirt when he saw one. However Steven liked what he saw. No classic slim pin up, but definitely his type, he considered.

"Take care now," and he turned to leave.

"Oh, he'll be well looked after."

"I meant you," Steven gave the briefest of winks and she wasn't one hundred percent sure if it ever existed. But it did, oh yes it definitely did. Steven smiled to himself as he found the exit.

"I quite like your friend, Ray." Lucy thought she was just talking to herself as she tidied his bed.

"Steven Blockley MP, that's who you might soon be dating." Ray opened one eye to see her flustered, yet undeniably pretty face.

## Chapter 42 April 1992

"Have you seen Ray?" Cyril was almost bursting at the seams. He was enquiring as to Ray's whereabouts upon the arrival of every punter.

"No, why?" Colin Sykes, 'Bill' to everyone, wondered what all the excitement was about.

"Look at this" and pointing to a minor headline on page six of his national newspaper, Cyril wanted to be the first to break the news to Ray.

Whilst not really 'schadenfreude', German for pleasure derived from the misfortune of others, Cyril wanted to be at the cutting edge of the delivery.

"I think he's out campaigning with Blocky" someone chirped in.

But Cyril needn't have bothered himself. Ray had already seen the article:

*'TRAGEDY AT SEX ORGY FARM'*

*'Police are still assessing the scene of what is being described as a terrible incident. A fourteen year old boy, believed to be the grandson of farm owner James Curzon, met with tragedy whilst playing in a barn at home yesterday. It is understood that he and a friend found medieval stocks hidden amongst the hay. They were thought to be used for sex games. Exact circumstances of death are yet to be determined, but it is believed that the boy was placed in them before tumbling from the height of the unsteady bales. No relatives of the boy were available for comment, but it is alleged that the farm is used as a regular venue for sex orgies. One neighbour who wished to remain anonymous said, "Everyone in these parts knows that*

*people come here from miles around to indulge their sexual fantasies." The coroner has been informed.*

If Ray was honest with himself, he would be first to admit he could muster no grief for James. However, outwardly his appearance displayed all the classic signs of shock. They were in 'Fat Frank's Cafe' enjoying a well earned break from canvassing when Ray himself flicked through the tabloid pages.

"You ok, Ray? You look like you've seen a ghost." Then twisting his neck to read the article from opposite, Steven immediately understood his friend's distress. A seldom discussed aspect of his life, Ray felt no desire to open up now and understanding this, Steven signalled the others to give Ray some space. Of course everyone knew of the rumours, but no one ever questioned or even goaded him for answers, as he might have done, if the roles were reversed.

"Come on, I'll take you home." Steven sympathetically patted Ray's shoulder.

"No, I'll carry on" Ray would not know what to do at home.

"It'll look better if you go Ray, don't let people think you don't care." Steven almost whispered his words.

"But that's the point, I don't even know James."

"Maybe not, but it will be better all round if you sign off for the day."

Ray understood what Steven was trying to get across, *'the campaign carried on with no concern for a dead son,'* the critics would have a field day. That and possible interruptions from the press would do Steven's cause no good at all.

"Ok, but I'd rather walk if you don't mind."

"Yes, the walk will do you good" Steven's words felt stupid, they had been walking all morning. "I'll call round later," he added in an effort to give his useless statement some credibility. Ray wanted to go to the pub, but which one? He knew most people secretly discussed the farm behind his back, so it was to be home, a bottle of scotch and possible oblivion.

Ray swore he had given up smoking for good. His lungs had taken a proper battering from the pneumonia. 'Stop smoking, cut down on the alcohol and eat a balanced diet,' his doctor had instructed him. But they had recovered now hadn't they? And after all, this latest trauma needed to be put in order and what better way than a good whisky and a consoling cigarette.

The clicking open of the sealed metal bottle top of the scotch and the removal of the clear film around the cigarette packet were like therapy to Ray. He knew it wasn't the answer, but he also knew he couldn't stop now. So by the time Steven arrived, he was indeed hammered and well into his second bottle. But most disturbing of all he had woken from a bad dream only to discover he had wet himself.

Quickly gathering his wits he called from inside without opening the door

"I'm ok, but I'm tired so I'm going to bed. I'll see you tomorrow if that's ok?" Ray tried not to stutter his words.

"You sure, Ray?" Steven was doubtful.

"Yeh, I just need to get my head down."

"Alright, I'll be round first thing." Steven stooped with his head close to the door in a way that somehow he hoped would make sound travel better through solid objects.

But Ray was already sliding down the hallway wall into a crouching position, he was sobbing uncontrollably, inside he was really hurt.

Ray found he woke from a fitful sleep in his own bed. Somehow he had managed to get himself there but could not remember the exact circumstances. Checking the bed and his nether regions he found there had been no repeat of yesterday's mishap. Picking up his cigarette packet he found it was empty; he had smoked all twenty. His delicate traumatised lungs confirmed the fact and yet he would have lit another, had there been one.

Gingerly dressing, he ached from head to toe; he hoped he wasn't coming down with a bout of flu or worse. Then the memory of picking himself up from a foetal position in the cold of the hallway in the small hours, might account for his condition.

Opening the curtains he saw Steven's car pull up. In the passenger seat sat Lucy, having the effect of lightening his mood somewhat. He was happy for his friend, more than anyone, he deserved to find true love. Taking a deep breath he opened the door on the second knock.

"Come in, the house is a bit of a mess, but what the hell, I had a drink, it won't be the first, it won't be the last." Ray held his hands up.

Not wanting to judge Ray's method of dealing with bad news, he simply asked,

"You ok?"

"Yeh, I got pissed for James and that's the end of it."

"Good, what are you going to do with yourself today?"

"I'm coming with you if that's ok?"

"Are you sure? People are talking about the farm."

"The farm's nothing to do with me. Yes, I fathered a child but I have no other connection, so if it doesn't reflect badly on you, having me along, I'd like to help."

"Get your coat, it's quite nippy." Steven smiled to his friend, whatever his plight he would always be there for him. "Lucy's coming along today." He decided to change the subject. "It's her day off."

"Yeh I've seen her, hey hey!" Ray fondly poked his fists in Steven's ribs in a manly tickling way. "I think you've cracked it there."

**Chapter 43** **April 9th 1992**

"What's wrong with everybody? How can a smug, fat bastard like him get re-elected? It just doesn't add up." It was only Ray's description, but his vocal opinion of the man who had beaten Steven into second place had left him outraged.

But the adding up had been done and the narrow loss was already being put down to, 'better the devil you know,' scenario.

'It's my fault' he told himself. 'People have put me, Steven and the farm episode all in one bag, so it's all down to me.' In truth, most people hadn't made any connection at all and quite rightly so. But what is now being described as 'dirty tactics' by Steven's main rival seemed to have made all the difference. Whilst not coming straight out with it, Geoffrey Charles MP hinted at some possible involvement or at least knowledge of 'illicit goings on.'

All opinion polls leading up to the election had Steven well in front, but by some miraculous coincidence, a television interview two days earlier replaced a 'lost cause' candidates screening.

Watching Angela as Steven dutifully congratulated the jubilant Mr. Charles, conveyed a message that probably signalled an end to their Thursday night sessions. This being the third one running that had been cancelled, the previous two put down to late evening canvassing. 'It was on the cards anyway,' he told himself. The once nimble, mind-blowing nymphomaniac's moves had become all too predictable.

It would be a shame though, having just 'quietly' celebrated her fifty-eighth birthday in Florida, she still looked fantastic. Good genes and a little help from quality make-up, a good hair stylist and her overall presence, helped her easily pass for ten years younger. But it was out of his hands, 'que sera sera' and all that shit.

But Ray's train of thought was rudely interrupted by a newspaper reporter with a photographer in tow, abruptly grabbing Steven's attention. "Steven, firstly can I offer you my commiserations on not gaining what on paper appeared a comfortable victory."

"Thank you," Steven naively replied.

"Do you think the outcome was swayed by the allegations that you may in some way be involved in the Curzon farm tragedy?" The reporter took no time in changing tack.

"Firstly, can I say I have no idea where the notion has arisen from, but I do offer my sympathies to the family involved."

"So you're adamant that you have no connection at all to the family?" he pushed.

"Absolutely none at all, I can unequivocally state, I have never met anyone in residence at that address."

"Mr. Blockley, you say you offer your sympathies to the Curzon family. Does that mean you condone the activities sometimes held at the farm?"

"All the details I am not privy to, I am sure will be dealt with by the police and coroner's inquest."

"If you had been successful tonight would you have been comfortable knowing such practices were happening in your constituency?"

"Surely that's a question for Mr. Charles, now if you'll excuse me." Steven held his composure when Ray was sure he himself would not have and offering inappropriate scant condolences he uttered,

"Tomorrow's fish and chip wrapping," in relation to the old saying about today's bad news.

"Yeh, tomorrow's fish and chip wrapping," Steven sighed.

Ray couldn't grasp Steven's true feelings, but other party supporters were not so guarded. He was an easy target as a direct result of the 'Charles camp' opportunist slur and he felt isolated. But one question was finally answered, that of his future as Angela's Thursday escape.

"Come on, that lot want blood and I want a good seeing to!"

**Chapter 44** **August 1992**

Being a creature of habit, disruptions to established routines doesn't usually bode well for Ray. 'Why tonight?' he asked himself, 'there are six other days in the week', why had Blocky chosen to ask him out to 'Napoli' tonight? The obvious answer was he wanted to see both he and Angela together, but Neville wouldn't have minded another night apart from his wife for the good of the party, surely?

All would be revealed, he was sure, but a swift couple in the White Lion would serve as an aperitif.

"Pint Ray?" Cyril's usual greeting saw Ray take his usual stool at the end of the bar.

But before he could take his first sip, a strange ringing sound started. It was coming from a smart suited business sort sat next to him, who then proceeded to take out a large mobile phone from a briefcase.

"Hello, Yeh, about an hour, love you too, bye."

Whilst not a complete unknown entity, Ray had never seen one in any of his regular haunts before.

"What's the world coming to?" he shook his head in disbelief.

"They're going to be the next big thing Ray." Cyril was ready to open up a debate on the subject.

"Bollocks! Would anybody really always want to be contactable? Honestly, why on earth would a bloke want his missus to be able to find him when he was out for a few?" He shook his head at the mere thought.

"No Ray, I tell you, everyone will have one in the not too distant future. I read an article in the paper only this week, now where is it?" Then he was off to search a pile of old newspapers to support his theory by finding the said article. "Here it is. It says less than one percent of people have a mobile phone today but by the year 2005, ninety percent of us will own one."

"Says who? Some newspaper columnist, who probably has a finger in the pie of some over ambitious phone company?" Ray was not convinced.

"I was down London last week and they're everywhere." Dennis found his cue to enter the latest teatime topic. "And what's hot in London today will be here tomorrow."

"He's right Ray, this writer says millions will be sold over the coming years." Cyril either believed the journalist or was just happy to fuel the now well underway discussion.

"You should make a stance now Cyril and ban them from the pub."

"Why's that Ray? I actually think they're a good idea." Cyril was now playing devil's advocate.

"Think about it, everybody's sat having a nice quiet pint, then ring ring everywhere. All your punters have been summoned home by their wives and you'll be sat here on your own twiddling your thumbs. You should be on your guard Cyril." Ray was pleased with his instant analysis.

"You've got a point there Ray, hadn't thought of that," and stating another worrying fact an air of gloom descended over the bar area. "The Joiners Arms has closed down, have you heard?"

"Yeh and the Punchbowl last month; I tell you, ban them mobile phones now."

"It's nothing to do with mobile phones." Dennis, now homing in on the topic, could only deal with facts.

"People just aren't going out anymore. They can't afford to; there's no employment down that side of town. It's just the tip of the iceberg mark my words. It will spread to here just like cancer."

"Thanks for cheering us up Dennis" Cyril solemnly remarked.

"Only pointing out the obvious" he defended his point of view.

"Well on that note, I'm off." Ray slid off his seat.

"Going somewhere nice? You're dressed pretty smart." Cyril's nosiness knew no bounds.

"I'm off to put a bomb in that mobile phone factory." Ray loved thwarting Cyril's prying.

"Put one in it for me!" he could hear being called from the inside as the door closed behind him.

The warm early evening air was thick with 'sugar steelers.' 'Why are they called that?' he asked himself again. Hadn't he once read that they are the white floaty seeds of the rosebay willow-herb? But his knowledge of nature was a bit sketchy. Taking his jacket off he threw it over his shoulder and with one finger through the coat hook, he once more took on the swagger of youth.

He hadn't even realised he was hungry until he opened the door of 'Napoli.' The air inside was a good ten degrees centigrade warmer than the humid evening outside. This had the effect of exaggerating the garlic, herbs and spices that mixed richly with the hot pizza bread aroma, giving an ambience of the sun-drenched Italian Riviera. Waiters sweated abundantly as they milled around from kitchen to restaurant. Ladies wafted table mats in conjunction with the ineffective ceiling fans, whilst red faced men found solace in cold beers.

"Over here Ray!" Steven spotted him before he had finished scanning the room.

"Cold beer please," he asked the unlikely named 'Giuseppe' before he even had chance to take his coat or drink order.

"Thirsty Ray?" Steven smiled.

"I'll say so; it's too hot for me." Ray blew upwards in order to signify cooling his brow.

"If I remember rightly, you're not too keen on the cold either."

"Yeh, no pleasing some people" Ray conceded.

Taking his seat he smiled flirtingly across at Lucy before unfittingly patting Angela's thigh. "Sorry I'm late." He considered inventing an excuse but figured it wouldn't wash in this company.

"We were starving so we've ordered some cheese and tomato garlic bread, is that ok with you?" Angela chirped in with cooling words, that Ray took to mean 'you're late, now sit down and behave.'

"Yeh fine, I'm starving too." Ray fell into line.

Ray knew what all this was about, though; Steven and Lucy's body language was a bit of a giveaway. And indeed the arrival of an upmarket champagne following pasta dishes and a tiramisu desert gave rise to the announcement.

"I want you to be the first to know, I've asked Lucy to marry me and can you believe this beautiful woman has agreed!" Then looking into each other's eyes, Ray and Angela knew they had the kind of love they could only dream of.

"Congratulations!" Ray stood to shake Steven's hand and lean across the table to kiss Lucy, followed by Angela also giving each an apt continental style embrace. It was then that they suddenly became aware that almost all the restaurant clientele were focusing attentions their way, but it was not the sight that intrigued them, it was the sound. Not for the first time today, Ray heard the head turning chords of a mobile phone.

"Sorry everyone, it's my phone, I better answer it." And reaching for a similar case to the suited pub drinker, Steven warily spoke into the handset.

"Hello... oh hi, is everything ok? ...Not at the moment. ...I see. ...Are you sure? Ok, bye, speak to you soon." At this point it seemed everyone in the room was waiting for an explanation from Steven.

"Is everything alright? Is it bad news? You look like you've had a shock" Angela curiously enquired.

Ray knew that these phones were bad news, but resisted the words of, 'not you as well?' It didn't seem appropriate just now.

"What's wrong? Has something bad happened?" Lucy was sincerely worried.

"It all depends on your interpretation of good or bad." Steven appeared a little stunned. "That was Mavis, she asked if I was watching the news."

"And?" Ray urged him to continue.

"Geoffrey Charles has collapsed and died on holiday in the south of France with his family."

"Oh!" it didn't seem like bad news to Ray,

"This means... there is going to be a bye-election." Angela finished Steven's words.

"Yes, a bye-election," finally finished the words himself."

Sensing Ray's growing realisation of the facts, Angela quickly whispered in his ear,

"Play it down, everyone's watching."

"Oh Yeh, with you now." Ray grasped the sensitive situation.

After all it wouldn't look good if one politician and his cronies took joy from the misfortune of another, now would it? But inwardly Ray was doing cartwheels for his friend.

## Chapter 45 October 1992

"I tell you, she is like a proper nympho."

"Are you not bothered she has been around most of your friends?" Derek Chapman was curious as to why he had no feelings of jealousy towards his latest girlfriend. But Ray quite liked young 'Sparko.' The teenage apprentice electrician reminded him of himself.

"Nah, she's not me proper bird, she takes two of us at once sometimes."

"Get away!" Derek was flabbergasted but didn't exactly move away from the growing group of listeners, in fact he was most keen to know more.

"Ere, look at this Polaroid of me and her, look what she's doing."

Ray being the first to gleefully examine the photograph quickly gulped the remainder of his beer down before making a quick exit. He didn't want to wait around for the outcome; the girl in question was Derek's daughter!

Chuckling to himself, 'shit, there'll be chaos in there in a minute' and he wasn't wrong. Sparko was off in the opposite direction 'quicksticks.' 'Ah well, back to the others.' He had a spring in his step that reflected no compassion for his fellow drinker's feelings.

Ray had skilfully split from Steven and his canvassing posse as they approached Church Street. He couldn't bear the thought of passing its several pubs without calling in at least one. With less than a week to the first bye-election since April's general, Ray needed a swift pint. Over the last fortnight, the town had become the nation's centre of attention. Journalists, reporters and TV cameras had flooded in. It was all becoming a bit of a pantomime and he was frightened to death of having a microphone pushed in his face. If he opened his mouth, he would surely put his foot in it, so to speak. Some of the candidates weren't so guarded though. Not that they needed to be; surely their chances were non-existent. The fourteen candidates saw all sorts; every conceivable party, along with independents, eccentrics and downright lunatics, one being the understated 'Screaming Lord Sutch.' Mind you, Ray quite liked one of his policies, that being, turning the pond in Man 'o the Moon Park into a wine lake, jumping on the back of a recent news item of European food-mountains and excess of grape. But just how many of the local half wits and imbeciles would actually take him on board was anyone's guess.

But the thing that Ray had trouble coming to terms with however was the fact that the main rival protagonist was to be David Hellier. Having narrowly lost his own seat, the well known ex-MP would now be travelling half way across the country to cynically contest somewhere he had never clapped eyes on or set foot in before.

"Surely they'll see through him?" Ray initially was confounded.

"Who?" Angela was only half listening.

"Well I don't mean the invisible man, do I? Him, David, anytime-anywhere, Hellier. The voters ain't gonna want an outsider are they?"

"I wouldn't be too sure Ray, he's a familiar face and people like what they know. This was a hard fought seat and they don't want to let it go." Steven bared the cold facts.

"Is it ok if I point out that fact when I talk to Joe Public?" Ray asked.

This was a difficult one for Steven, he knew Ray could be a loose cannon and he sure wasn't going to play dirty.

"We'll point out the benefits of having a local MP and how we understand our own community."

"Ok." Ray appeared to accept, but in secret he would whisper in certain discerning voters' ears that Mr. Hellier is known as the Martini man, 'Anytime, anywhere, anyplace, is that what we want?' And to be fair it was working, at least to his face it was. People agreed they didn't want an outsider. He knew folk often went along with whoever knocked on their door, but if Ray believed half of them, then they were onto a winner.

And indeed it was when the red-face infiltrator appeared on late night television that the interviewer asked if he knew of his new nickname. His circular spiel laughed off the comment, but he was inwardly annoyed that such a simple slur could have taken hold.

"Is that what they call him?" Ray casually uttered.

"Hmmm." Steven had a good idea where it might have originated. But all is fair in love and war and after all, this is a sort of war, isn't it?

There was an air of resignation amongst the unruly line up of candidates; most knew their fate as they had no real expectations to begin with; but as the result unfolded, the realisation of not only not winning, but being pushed into third place was a bitter pill for David Hellier to swallow. At least he wasn't overtaken by the Monster Raving Loony party! That was one thing to be thankful for, although their 749 votes were not to be sniffed at. But it was now time to move on and concentrate on his many business concerns.

"I'm just not wanted here." David Hellier understood it was now the right moment to call time on his political career.

"Thanks for all you've done Ray; once again, I am in debt to you. You're really good with people. You should try your hand at local politics." Steven looked almost teary, but Ray put it down to the euphoria of winning.

"What me, nah. I know what I know and nowt else."

"Don't put yourself down Ray, it doesn't do you justice. And anyway, what kind of comment is that? I know what I know and nowt else? That's just about everyone in the world isn't it?"

"I suppose so, if you look at it like that, Yeh. So what happens next?"

"Well in the next few days I will take up position in the House Of Commons. I'll make an introductory speech and take it from there." If Ray was honest, Steven looked a little terrified of the prospect, but didn't comment on the fact.

"Bloody hell, this is one in the eye for those crap teachers at school, isn't it?" Ray smiled fondly at his friend.

"Yeh, but the potential is there for all of us, it's just a matter of self-belief, channelling our positive energy and best assets into our ambitions."

Ray smiled, he knew what Steven was saying, but for him, himself, a simple life was all he needed.

"Right, I've just got a few more handshakes, and then I'll be back. You asked what happens next. Well for the more immediate future, we're going back to mine; that positive side of me put some champagne on ice."

**Chapter 46** **New Years Eve 1999**

"You know the year 2000 will actually be the one hundredth year of the twentieth century, the real millennium will be next year," Dennis matter-of-factly stated.

"Oh right, we'll tell the world to put the celebrations on hold shall we?" It was the first Ray had heard that anyone didn't consider this, the 'big one.'

"And it's just possible that technology will crash at midnight, it is thought the 'millennium bug' could affect computers worldwide."

"A right barrel of laughs you are tonight." Dennis could be a pain in the arse sometimes and Ray didn't have a problem letting him know his take on killjoy behaviour.

"Only letting you know the facts, do you want me to explain why it's not this year?"

"No! Just enjoy the evening and get pissed." Barry backed up Ray in quashing Dennis' downer on the fast approaching new decade that it was now thought would be known as the 'noughties.'

But the thing that was annoying Ray lately was the taking for granted that people would be enjoying a full life into whatever term you applied the fast approaching turn of midnight.

"Ray Taylor, it's Ray Taylor next... come on Ray." The DJ greeted Ray with a beaming smile and handing him the microphone, he soon realised the up and coming singer was no stranger to the stage. It was around three years ago that he found he could sing along to the fast growing popularity of the karaoke. The talent of singing might be a little strong, but Ray found crooning the old classics was a breeze and indeed his rendition of one of his own favourites, 'Gentle on my Mind,' in the style of Dean Martin left the drunken connoisseurs of music chanting for more. It was the main reason Ray had chosen to spend this auspicious occasion at the Bridge Street Working Men's Club and the alcohol-infused audio sensory organs of the clientele had been well and truly altered. Cheering on the good, the bad and the downright ugly vocal chords of the willing and press-ganged singers; all had one eye on the clock, fast ticking towards the hour of much speculation.

Sitting back down, he cringed at the sound of some ageing woman behind him, who for some reason appeared to be dressed in her daughter's little black miniskirt, murdering 'I Will Survive.'

"Jeeesus, what does she sound like?" Ray winced.

"Never mind that, what does she look like?" Barry exclaimed.

And turning around to make eye contact with the woman, Ray found he was being given the 'glad eye' or at least one of them. The other was not quite in tune with its partner, so to speak.

"You're in there Ray." Dennis seemed a little more cheery.

"What, with Mrs. Football Pools eyes over there?" Ray shot a quick retort.

"What do you mean?" Dennis was not always quick to grasp the moment.

"Football pools, one home, one away." Ray was pleased with his sharp wit.

"All the same, she wants to play away with you Ray." Barry was not to be left out of the banter.

"Mutton dressed as lamb," Dennis eyed her with disapproval.

"Mutton dressed as mutton, more like it." Barry piped up.

"Ten, nine, eight...come on altogether... three, two, one! Happy new millennium!" The DJ announced in his best, would-be radio voice.

Then an excess of kisses and an excuse for quick gropes followed, ensuring an inebriated yet joyous gathering. But the most noticeable difference from that of bygone years was the immediate shift to calls and messages being exchanged on mobile phones.

"Bloody mobile phones," Ray muttered, yet there was one in his pocket delivering its content at that very moment. He positively did not want one and indeed had trouble understanding its workings, but Angela had insisted, 'I may need to get hold of you or pass on a message.' So under the circumstances, Ray had relented.

"How does this bloody thing work?" he cursed as he fumbled with the buttons that were far too small. Extending the phone to arms length to try and focus, he gave up and handed it to Dennis. "What's happening with it? It's beyond me."

"You've got a message, oh no, wait a minute, you've got two, another's just come through."

"Read it to me, I'll never understand them things."

"It's from Blocky; it says *'Happy New Year from Steven, Lucy and the twins.'"*

"Ah, brilliant, can you send a reply from me? 'Reciper... Returning my best wishes'" Rays words were beginning to slur.

"Give me a minute, I'll get the next message up for you first... it's from Angela, it says..." but Dennis' voice tailed off before relaying the message. "You better try and read this yourself Ray; it's not for my eyes."

"Bloody hell, I'm going to have to get some glasses," Ray cursed. Then using all his concentration, he brought the words into focus.

*'Hi Ray, its Neville. Just to let you know that Angela passed away before the stroke of midnight. She sent you her love, will speak to you soon.'*

Out of the corner of his eye Ray could see Dennis putting his finger to his lips in order to signal Barry to stay silent. He guessed he had already given him the news that was only meant for his own attention. Of course everyone knew of Ray and Angela's relationship, but this revelation was totally out of the blue to all but close friends and family.

Angela had been diagnosed with stomach cancer in September and its aggression had ravaged her liver and other organs before treatment could even begin. Being one of the first people to be told of the inevitability, he was instructed to get on with his life. It wasn't easy. Angela was the nearest thing to a permanent partner Ray had ever had. Most probably its longevity could be put down to the casual format and simplicity of their friendship. And a friend she was indeed, "and I'm gonna drink to my friend," Ray muttered to himself as he headed glassy-eyed to the bar.

Ray's head hurt, his mouth was rancid and he wasn't quite sure of his whereabouts. Slowly it all started coming back to him as he turned to see a sleeping woman at his side; if he thought his mouth was bad, this person's was off the scale, putrid. Her eyes were closed but he knew exactly what lay beneath her tightly shut lids. He felt sick, not because of the vast quantity of consumed alcohol, not because he had slept with the anti-Christ of female singers, but he felt he had trashed the memory of Angela. He knew why he had done it though, it was the only way he could handle stressful situations; oblivion, angry sex or both. In this case it was the latter and his vague memory of robotic thrusting left him with bile rising from his stomach.

Throwing back the bed sheets, the woman, whose name he didn't know, began to stir,

"You're not going are you? I'm ready for a bit more fun." But now being caught between finding the bathroom and looking back over his shoulder, he threw up on his own pile of hastily disregarded clothes. "Well you won't be putting them on, will you?" and slipping out of the sheets, she screwed her face as she gathered them up. "I'll put them in the wash for you. You go and clean yourself up."

Feeling a tinge of guilt, Ray realised for the first time that he was engaging with another human being. He was so used to selfishly indulging his own needs; he would normally walk straight away from such an encounter. But he was here for the duration of a wash and dry cycle at least.

"I'll put the kettle on, and don't worry Ray; I'll take last night for what it was." There was an immediate understanding; Pam or Pammy Roach had seen it all before. She knew she was no beauty; in fact the world was often a cruel place for her. But her figure was ok and she was well known for her wicked sense of humour, so all in all, she got by.

"There's a robe hung behind the door." Ray could hear Pammy call as she descended the stairs.

Touching the fabric of the towelling robe as he entered the kitchen, Ray raised an eyebrow as to ask who the owner was, obviously not her own. He wondered about the male occupant of the household. He wasn't in the mood for an unwelcome conflict should its usual incumbent return unannounced.

"Callum, my son, he's at uni; he came back for Christmas, but apparently an un-missable party was taking place in Sheffield last night."

Joining Pam at the table he gave her a weak smile.

"Ouch!" Pammy touched her jaw as to indicate a sore tooth. "Bloody toothache, my back molar has cracked and it hurts and tastes like shit, but the dentist isn't open 'til Tuesday; sorry if I got a bit close."

"Well that accounts for one thing," Ray silently conceded.

"Neither of our gobs would be in the best of order after last night" Ray felt his reply was nothing short of magnanimous by his standards.

"If you don't mind me asking, was something wrong last night? But it's just that you seemed to get upset in an angry sort of way."

"Sorry, it's nothing." Ray wanted no sympathy.

"You sure? You also had a bad dream, did you know?"

"It's a friend that's all, she died yesterday." It already felt like an age ago.

"Angela Charlton?" Pammy guessed.

"Yes, how did you know?" Ray was a little taken aback.

"It's not much of a secret that you two had a thing going on. Anyway I'm sorry." Pammy looked genuine.

"It's ok, life goes on." Ray appeared philosophical.

"And last night I really pounced on you. You must have been hurting inside, I'm sorry, I was being selfish. But I wasn't about to let you go, the cobwebs needed shifting down below, so to speak." Pam tried to make light of their encounter. "Oh, that's the washer finished, I'll put them in the dryer, should be about half an hour, is that ok?"

"Yeh, that's ok." Ray had resigned himself to the wait; anyway there was nothing to rush home for. "What do people say about me and Angela? Or more correctly, what did they say?" Ray assumed gossip of the relationship was now past tense.

"Not a lot really, it was more taken for granted. I don't think it was common knowledge she was poorly though, I saw her a few weeks ago and if I'm honest, I might have guessed. Cancer wasn't it?"

"Yes."

"Thought so! I usually have a feel for such things."

"Well if you get a 'feel' about me, I'd rather not know." Psychics and the likes spooked Ray.

However during the thirty minute duration of the tumble dry he decided he quite liked Pam. But his shallow side would probably not allow him to be associated with Pammy's not so aesthetic appearance. Maybe he might call around sometimes on the sly, he considered.

"I think these are dry now, do you want me to iron them?"

"No it's ok, you've done enough." Ray now felt slightly mothered.

"Should be ok anyway, most of the creases have fallen out."

As he dressed, Pammy realised she was staring and had to consciously avert her eyes. She longed to have a man around the house again, but knew Ray would never be a permanent fixture.

"Call again Ray; you know, if you fancy a brew or a chat." She thought she should say more but it might appear a little desperate.

"Yes, thanks." But at this stage, Ray didn't know if he ever would and Pammy's instinct was probably not. All her life she'd made light of her looks. Ernie, her ex-husband, no Brad Pitt himself, would cruelly joke 'don't go out to the milkman, you'll turn his load sour,' or similar to pub landlords about their beer. So yes, Pammy Roach had no great expectations of ever laying out slippers on a winter's evening for Ray Taylor.

"Bye Ray." Pammy handed Ray his coat from the hat stand and in reply he gave a small nod before turning to exit the small terrace. As the door closed behind him he took a quick look around to see if he'd been spotted, before habitually placing his thumbs and forefingers to raise his collar against the elements.

**Chapter 47 January 11th 2000**

'If they dropped it, would it split open, revealing its content in front of everyone?' Ray was in an almost childlike daydream state. 'Does everyone have that thought?' he silently wondered to himself. 'Is it normal to think that?' he challenged his own imagination. 'Probably not, it's only my brain that would pop up with that question.'

Then fetching his focus back to the vision of the four pallbearers shuffling along with Angela's casket, Ray realised his hands were freezing cold. Clasping them tightly in quick succession he then blew his breath into them in an effort to raise their temperature, before taking his position in the procession, filing silently into the chapel. He hated this place, it brought him no comfort and the sermons of the preachers always felt cold and empty. Oh yes, they would think they had successfully delivered their words to the grieving families, but what did they know of the real Angela or his mother? Ray's anger was building inside. He assumed today would be mournful but he was bitter about the whole cynicism of it all.

He then saw her! Angela that is, not as herself in her last days, but a ten years younger version.

"You ok Ray?" a voice that seemed detached from reality was asking, but he felt faint and was sure he was about to keel over.

"It's Angela's sister, over from Canada."

"What?" Ray began to gather his composure.

"Deborah, you were looking at Deborah, She's a ringer for her isn't she?" Steven quietly informed him.

"Shit Yeh, I thought I'd seen a ghost." Ray laughed at his own stupidity, at least his mood had lightened a little, and that's the way he wanted it to stay. His mind was firmly made up. He would show no emotion; it wasn't the manly thing to do blub or get all teary. He would not listen to the heart wrenching words that would surely flow in abundance; they might make him deviate from the plan to stay impenetrable.

Instead he remembered a story he'd heard from a gravedigger and might even adapt it to be one of his own later at the wake. 'At a nearby church cemetery, a grave had been dug and was awaiting the recently deceased. However at the moment of internment, it was found to be a fraction too small. Hurriedly sending for the excavator, the vicar instructed its driver to lengthen the hole. But by the fact of the closeness of neighbouring plots, the machine encroached on the next one in line, exposing an open ended coffin. To the horror of the grieving family, the feet of the occupant were revealed, still wearing his final resting place slippers. The price tag of £4.99 still proudly displayed, it was indeed a good advert for the local discount store.'

Whether or not there is any truth in the story is anyone's guess, but amongst council employees the story is passed on as recent folklore.

Ray suddenly became aware that he was being watched, his smiling at that exact moment was not appropriate, it seemed.

"Just fondly remembering Angela," he whispered to the woman next to him, but the realisation that

Neville had broken down in tears reading, 'A Poem To Be Read At My Funeral,' written by Angela herself, had gone unnoticed by Ray. "Sorry," Ray winced through clenched teeth.

Steven had now taken over the recital from the grief stricken Neville. Looking around, the place was awash with tears but Ray was somehow glad he hadn't listened to the four verses of poetry. He was proud of his stoic deafness.

Making a beeline for Deborah back at Neville's, Ray was fixated by her presence.

"Ray, Ray Taylor." He offered her his hand and what he considered was his cutest smile.

"Deborah Livingstone, I'm Angela's sister." Her Canadian accent showed no traces of ever living in England.

"I was Angela's... friend," Ray searched for what he hoped was the right word.

"Yes I've heard. Angela and I were in constant contact by email."

Ray was quite astounded that news of their relationship had travelled the Atlantic.

"Do you know you look exactly like her when we first met?" Ray moved a little closer and although not exactly whispering, it was toned down enough to up the ante in the flirting stakes.

"Yes, it's been said many times but there is a big age difference; there's nineteen years between us," Deborah informed him stepping back a little.

"Nineteen years, wow." Ray was considering a kid sister replacement would be an ideal prospect.

"Our parents were twenty and nineteen when they had Angela, I suppose I was unplanned, but the world's full of us I assume, mistakes that is."

"You look like no mistake to me," Ray again stepped closer. "Do you think we could move on to somewhere a little quieter? I mean, after the wake." Ray put his cards on the table, with his best tried and tested cheeky grin.

"Have you ever been to Canada Ray?"

"No, why?" he was curious. 'Was this an invite?' he wondered.

"Well it's full of what I call men's men; you know, hunks, lumberjacks, that sort of thing."

"Yes?" Ray didn't know where this was going.

"So what makes you think I would take up with my sister's bit on the side? When was the last time you looked in a mirror? Oh yes, you've had your moments no doubt, but the lines on your face can only be described as craggy; you stink like an old ashtray and of last night's booze. So Ray, I don't think I'll go for Angela's excuse for hot sex if you don't mind."

"So that's definitely a no is it?" Although like a punch in the stomach, he admired her feistiness.

"You know Ray, my sister hasn't been reduced to ashes yet and you try a stunt like this! I hope she's looking down in disgust, not that I believe in that sort of thing."

Ray became aware that not for the first time today, he was under observation.

"Only trying to be friendly." He began to back off in an effort to save grace. Looking around, several pairs of eyes had taken in the encounter and none were favourable. Taking hold of his tumbler of scotch, he downed it in one before taking his leave.

Closing the door behind him, he then put his coat on with his customary collar flick as he walked for the last time down Neville's driveway. He felt angry and humiliated now his rebuff had sunken in and he could only think of regaining his stupid pride in one way.

"It's gonna have to be Pammy," he muttered to himself. "At least that's a given," and the fifteen minute walk would help him compose himself, but it was not to be. No one was in at the modest two up two down. Turning back his cuff, his watch glared back in the weak watery winter sunshine. It was two-thirty. She would be at work and would probably be there for some time yet. For the first time in years, Ray felt totally alone in the world. He had always looked forward to his Thursdays. Admittedly, the sex had stopped some months earlier but Angela was still in his world. But now he had no one, not a soul and for the first time, the brutal reality hit home. 'Old and craggy' but Ray realised something else; all he wanted was to cuddle up to someone in a primitive childlike way.

## Chapter 48 March 2007

It was day four of filming and Ray was somewhat dismayed by the slow pace of progress. The clique made up of youth and experience were a mysterious lot, indeed these people were a totally different breed, this 'television set.'

The production, if ever finished, was to be sixth of six in a series of documentaries, entitled 'what's happened to our...' Ray was informed, the previous five being 'high street,' 'schools,' 'industry.' 'hospitals,' and 'youth.' So if all went to plan, 'what's happened to our pubs,' would air in conjunction with the smoking ban on July 1st later this year.

Ray had been nominated by Cyril as a 'pub character' and it might have been considered an honour were it not for the others similarly chosen. Ronnie Evans, one notch above tramp status had spent every spare penny in 'the Griffin' and as a consequence had a seat named after him in 'Ronnie's corner.' Marjorie O'Connor had a similar background, spending forty years as a local prostitute and was now ending her years as a permanent fixture in 'the Spread Eagle.' Without a tooth to her name, she was still known to turn the odd trick in this, her seventy-fifth year!

Rays interview was to take place on a Monday but tighter schedules of others concerning the plight of the British pub had taken preference. A spokesman for a major brewing chain was followed by the owner of a micro brewery. Terry Fletcher was drafted in to replace Cyril at the last minute to represent landlords. Nerves it seemed had got the better of him, but his official excuse was a bout of gout. A representative of 'Camra', R.A.T.S. (Real Ale Tasting Society) and a religious type spouting on about the evils of alcohol were all deemed higher in the pecking order than the humble drinker. The silver lining however was free beer or more likely paid for by the TV Company for those kept waiting.

The Pack Horse, despite its rural location was to represent a struggling town centre pub. Clever editing would show scenes of Church Street and its pubs whilst internal shots would be taken at the country venue. Ray understood the logic, the entourage of technical units and catering vehicles would entirely block the narrow thoroughfare.

"Ok we're ready for you now Ray." A young woman, 'no a girl' Ray corrected himself, beckoned him over. The lesbian sort greeted him with a fixed smile on her face.

"If you just take a seat where the camera is facing." A pint of beer was awaiting his arrival and was his prop it seemed.

"Take a slurp of your beer Ray, act natural, as if this is your local, then we'll begin."

Suddenly realising he was totally out of his comfort zone, Ray felt anything but natural. His heart was pounding. 'Calm down,' he told himself, 'it's just stage nerves.'

"You ok Ray?" A voice called out, but he couldn't identify its source. The vast amounts of equipment along with far too many bodies confused the whole scene.

"Yes." He took a deep breath and tried to ignore the tense pains in his chest. Someone came alongside and padded his brow with make-up.

"You'll be ok Ray; it's quite daunting in front of a camera isn't it? Just take your time." The sound of the woman's soft words eased the tension a little. 'His blood pressure had been raised, that's all,' he told himself. But before he knew it, they were underway, 'what happened to the lights, camera, action?' Maybe he missed the cue.

"How do you think the smoking ban will affect the way pubs are run?" the interviewers familiar voice asked. After a short pause, Ray considered, 'that's no simple question' but with a sip of his beer he began.

"I don't think it will last." He finally conquered his nerves.

"What do you mean by that?"

"Well I think after six months or so the government will reverse its decision."

"Why do you say that?" The interviewer decided to keep it simple. His initial question had been deviated from.

"Well some pubs are already struggling and come winter, who's gonna want to go outside for a fag?"

"So you think the ban will only be temporary?"

"Yes."

"The smoking ban aside, why do you think so many pubs are closing down?"

"Cheap booze at the supermarkets, and immigration."

"I understand cut prices in the stores, but what do you mean by 'immigration?'" The interviewer perked up a little.

"Well there are certain areas in this and other similar towns that have given way to non-alcohol consuming communities." Ray was searching his brain for political correctness.

Somewhat disappointed, the interviewer would have preferred a more colourful answer.

"Doesn't it upset you that an immigrant population are somehow dictating the closure of public houses?"

Ray knew where this was going; he was being lured into a trap.

"Its supply and demand, so they will have to bow to the inevitable where those areas are concerned." Ray was quite pleased with his political style stance.

"Don't you resent that your choices are somewhat limited?"

"Oh yes, but I can't make people get off their backsides and go to the pub can I?"

"And you think that's all is needed; get off their backsides and patronise the local pub?"

"No, unemployment and low pay are major factors."

The interviewer realised he wasn't going to achieve the desired effect of drawing Ray into blaming the Muslim community for the closures. They could possibly play around with the editing at a later date.

"So going back to my initial question, I asked how do you think the smoking ban will affect the way pubs are run?"

"I think more will close, unless they fight the ban. I do however see a future with a limited number of pubs in our towns. I'm tired of trying to remember the names that have been taken over by funeral directors, fast food outlets, or are now empty spaces where they have been demolished. Our heritage is fast disappearing."

"Cut!" someone behind the camera called.

"Ok Ray, that's great, I think we have enough."

Not exactly what the production team, or more to the point, what one particular person, wanted. They would have to see what the cutting room could come up with. At least the other two characters didn't disappoint.

Ray wasn't sure what to make of it all, to be honest. It was all a bit overwhelming. He knew at one point they tried to sway his opinion, but his time around Steven had taught him how to steer clear of certain issues.

But it was the chest pains which momentarily came to the forefront of his thoughts. They were becoming more and more frequent, especially under any sort of exertion. 'Ah, it'll be alright' he said to himself. 'I'll cut back on the cigs, which should sort it.' A visit to the doctors apparently never even entered his head.

Sitting bolt upright in bed that night, 'bloody hell, that's it!' Something had been bugging Ray all day. 'It was him!' The more he thought about it, the more he was convinced. His interview earlier was supposed to be nothing more than his take on the town centre pubs, but it had turned into some kind of grilling.

Now he knew why he had been chosen to take part. His moment in the spotlight had been conducted by the same person who interviewed Steven on the night of his first election. That evening he gunned for blood for some kind of involvement at the farm, but what was his reasoning? He didn't fall for the trap, there was no ammunition gained so why would anyone go to all that trouble? 'Ah well, whoever you are, you didn't out fox Ray Taylor.' Turning over he went back to sleep quite pleased with himself that he'd foiled this character assassin's plan.

**Chapter 49** **January 2009**

"Don't worry Ray; it happens to all men at some point in their lives."

"What are you, a fucking expert on men's erection problems all of a sudden?" Ray was angry and could feel his blood pressure rising, the tightness in his chest was confirmation.

"No, I'm not a fucking expert, as you put it, but it's not hard to imagine that everyone will have a problem in that department sometimes." Pammy's sympathy for Ray's macho ego was wearing thin. He had shown little in the way of assurances for her present plight.

"Exactly, it's not hard, that's the fucking problem."

"What about Viagra? You could go and see the doctor?" Pam offered the perfect solution and these bouts of breathlessness and chest pains could be looked into at the same time, she hoped.

"No, I know someone who is selling a similar product down the pub; he imports it from China or somewhere like that." But Ray's dilemma would be how to ask for it without revealing he was struggling to 'get it up.' He remembered... well he couldn't quite recall who, but boy did that guy get some stick when everyone learnt of his inabilities. 'Keep your pecker up, everything will be ok' or 'keep a stiff upper lip old boy, something might as well be,' were amongst the ribbings the person, whose name would come to him in a minute, had received.

But deep down inside, Ray knew the real problem; it was Pammy, it was her fault he couldn't get a hard on. No real turn on at the best of times, but all this moping around at losing her job at Woolies was getting him down. About seventy men and women had been told of redundancies at the local Woolworths just before Christmas and any hope of a takeover was now out of the question. 'Bloody hell, she could get another job, but could he face life without...' well it wasn't worth thinking about. So a plan was now in place to prove to himself that it was just a minor hiccup and normality would soon return under the right circumstances.

Exactly why this particular location was chosen, Ray couldn't quite remember. He felt once he'd made his initial enquiry, all the terms and conditions were out of his hands. Standing in the reception at the Midland Hotel situated on the seafront at Morecambe, he could understand how a certain type of person would marvel at its architecture. The pristine art deco building had been meticulously restored to its former glory to an almost fastidious standard.

One thing he could recall however, was by taking the trouble to make the journey himself, would save £150 in travel expenses. Hell it only cost £16 on the train. In this game it is think of a figure and double it, or so it would appear.

Melissa, probably not her real name, had agreed to meet Ray here; she being local to the area would now not have to travel any distance. He'd chosen the petite blond after contacting 'Wishes' escort agency in Manchester and after paying their fee and agreeing the rest with the girl herself. By tomorrow morning he would be £600 worse off.

Yes, he could have gone elsewhere; he knew where girls plied their trade locally and it would have saved him a small fortune, but he also knew what standard of health and hygiene could be expected. 'No, this was the right decision' he told himself. With the right woman, in the right environment, all his fears of impotence would soon be dispelled.

"Hi, you must be Ray."

"Yes." Ray stood up to face the twenty-one year old student who was closer to thirty, but stunning never the less.

"Melissa," and holding her hand out, she warmly shook Rays, this was business after all.

"Can we have a drink in the rotunda bar first and get the formalities out of the way?" and in nodding her head away from the reception area to the far end of the hotel, would mean removing themselves from view of the hotel management. Establishments of any repute will not knowingly tolerate transactions of this nature it seems. "Do you have..." another unwritten rule apparently is to make only a suggestion of money.

"Oh yes" and handing a white envelope over Ray quietly mouthed the words, "check it."

"I'll just go and powder my nose and if everything's ok, the night's yours," and with a warm smile she smoothly left Ray to ponder the possibilities.

'Shit, she may have just done a bunk with my money,' Ray began to panic. 'She could be hurtling down the seafront in a getaway car, how naive could I be?

But just as his pulse rate was about to go off the scale she returned with a fond smile and a new coat of lipstick?'

"Do you want a drink?" Ray asked. He sure could do with one himself.

"Your call Ray, but if you're having one, mine's a G and T."

Returning from the bar, Ray wanted to ask all the questions he supposed everyone in the same position would. Why this lifestyle? Is she single or is there a man sat at home twiddling his thumbs, wondering where the money comes from? He could go on but what was the point? Whatever her reasons, she was here and heavily compensated.

"So Ray, we can talk if you want or we can just go up to your room if you'd rather?"

But every time Ray thought of any relevant topics of conversation, nothing left his lips; she would only tell him what he wanted to hear anyway, he figured.

"I think we'll go up." He was not really in the mood to be humoured.

Melissa sat on the end of the bed and kicked off her expensive looking shoes. Her skirt riding up a little revealed a glimpse of a stocking top and at this sight Ray hoped for first stirrings within his loins. 'Hello, brain to cock? Woman in need of your services.' He silently tried to kick start his animal instincts, but the word 'flop' again reared its ugly head.

Touching the top button of her blouse, Melissa stood motionless before seductively undoing them in sequence giving view to an expensive uplifting lacy bra. Ray wasn't sure whether the smooth of her breast had received a little help or not, but it had been a while since he had seen such perfect specimens. Then, as if to answer his question, she unhooked her bra, exposing them with virtually no gravity fed movement south.

"Just going to shower, I would prefer you did the same."

On hearing those words, Rays next thought should really have been of Angela, however it was of the glittering moisturising cream applied to her chest and shoulders that would now be washed away. But Ray needn't have bothered; the showering scenario was mainly for Melissa's assurances as to her client's cleanliness. So as he dutifully returned from his five minutes under the hot water jets, Melissa sat under covers, nipples tantalisingly unexposed, but sparkling body cream still intact. The bed sheet appeared to have been purposely smoothed down and arranged around her body shape, as if for some form of tease.

As for Melissa, she had seen it all before and looking at the naked man before her, knew what all this was about. He had a need to prove his manhood in these, his autumn years. Her instant assessment was one of a man who once had it all, in the bedroom at least, but from her point of view, this was an all too familiar occurrence and her hard core inner self could no longer pity these egotistic stereotypes. As for now, from experience she has two options.

1: See the night through; let the punter fumble like a virgin schoolboy, thrusting his midriff where an erection should be, in vain attempts to miraculously harden, ending in blubbering like a baby. Or

2: Cut a deal, hand some cash back and be home in bed by ten. But private school fees are a worry and the bills won't pay themselves, so option 1 will have to suffice for now.

But it seems, a third option would now have to be added for future reference. This, her latest client knew no shame and would not be showing an outburst of emotion at his failure. Her instincts usually steered her clear of anything other than the 'compliant' types; men who knew their place and were just generally happy, to be in the company of a beautiful woman. Younger, good looking men were not fazed by her looks and may even have similar sat at home. Their sex drive was likely to be insatiable and whilst occasionally welcome, older failures were preferable.

"How about a striptease? You know, a bit of dancing and titillation?" Ray chanced his arm.

"Sorry Ray, I'm not a stripper or some kind of burlesque dancer; our deal was a straight basic evening." Melissa hoped there would be no trouble.

"Well what does that entail? It's all a bit vague isn't it?"

"Straight sex, oral or hand relief, always with the use of a condom, nothing kinky or sado." Melissa knew some of the other girls at this stage would expand their portfolio and offer much, much more, at an extra cost of course. Some knew no bounds and could leave with upwards of £2000, but at what price to health and wellbeing? It was not one she herself was willing to pay.

Melissa wrongly imagined that when some amount of satisfaction had been given, she would be able to slope off, once he had given way to slumber. But Ray was ahead of her.

"Come on then, let's see what you can do under the 'straight rules.' Then if all else fails, I'll wait for the 'morning horn.'" Even under the present circumstances, Ray sometimes awoke with an early morning erection and that was not going to be wasted.

But satisfaction didn't arise in the way Ray would have hoped, either by evening, or with the dawn of light.

"Limp, lifeless bastard, useless!" he cursed. Still Melissa couldn't muster much in the way of sympathy; it had all unfolded in the way she preferred anyway. Money bagged with minimal prostitution of her own body; a good night at the office was had.

As she closed the door behind her, Ray closed his eyes with what he now realised was embarrassment.

"What's wrong with me?" 'Is this it? A useless piece of anatomy now, with only one purpose for the rest of my natural? I can raise my hand, my leg, anything but a hard on! Have I finally descended to the point in my life where I reach for my pipe and slippers and find comfortable slacks appealing? Fuck me, I feel like shooting myself.' What some men come to terms with as a matter of fact had the effect of leaving Ray at an extremely low ebb.

"Perhaps Pammy's right, that I need some help after all." But to go back and admit she was correct went against the grain. "Shit, how do I go about putting it right?"

Ray checked out without eating breakfast, he couldn't stomach it. He felt empty and hollow but food wasn't the answer. The bright winter sunshine brought no warmth as he walked along the promenade. Most of the shops, cafes and tourist attractions were closed. For most, there would be no point in opening, only the odd jogger or cyclist had bothered to venture out. An icy wind bit into his cheeks and ears as it found its way across the open bay, unobstructed until it found land, this side of the Irish Sea. His decision to cross the road for some kind of refuge left him with a further chill. There facing him was the tiny shop of a gypsy fortune teller. He felt as though he had been sent by the north wind that still stung his skin, to find out what fate had in store for him.

"Bollocks to that!" Ray shivered. 'She'll probably tell me something I don't want to hear.' Doctors, nurses, psychics, what did it matter? They would all probably suck in a sharp intake of breath like a dodgy car dealer when announcing the inevitability of a vehicle's demise, so no, not today thanks.

Ray had no idea for how long he had walked on auto pilot and had no recollection of his route to his present location. But he now found he was absent-mindedly staring into the window of what appeared to be some kind of backstreet herbalist shop. Shaking his head in conjunction with another shiver, he muttered

"What's happening? This is really weird."

But just as he was just about to walk away, the old fashioned sound of a shop doorbell rang. An elderly

Oriental lady, the smallest he had ever seen, exited, but as she did so, held the door open for Ray to enter.

The words 'no, I'm not going in' were supposed to leave his lips, but in some strange way, didn't.

Peering into the dimly lit interior after the bright of the sunshine, gave the effect of viewing into the past like some Dickensian curiosity shop. But in an odd way for Ray who is usually spooked at anything eerie or out of the ordinary, the place felt quite welcoming. In another life it would have been a wondrous sweet shop with the jars filled with all manner of childhood delights. Or better still, a tobacconist's from a bygone era, where the contents would have been those exotic brands that surround the mystique of the aromatic pipe smoker. This thought instantly took Ray back to his childhood in his grandparent's home, where the delightful smells filled every room and beyond, into the street on a summer's day. But the only source of heat today in the cluttered room full of a mysterious montage of tins, glass containers and boxes was a three bar electric fire.

"Mr. Scorpio, come on in," a small Oriental man only marginally taller than the woman leaving, beckoned him in. Looking around for another customer who must have entered behind him, Ray realised he was alone in venturing forward.

"Mr. Scorpio, Scorpio your horoscope, yes?" The man again spoke assumingly, referring to the fact that Ray was born under that star sign.

"Yes." This would normally have sent him packing, but there seemed no harm in the man guessing what was a one in twelve shot.

Then smiling, the man returned to some undefined duties, leaving Ray to browse. He wondered if the woman who was leaving the premises was his wife and if so, had they destined further generations of children and grandchildren to this mini person gene?

"How can I help you sir?" the man brought Ray back from his speculation.

"Oh... er... I just wondered if..." Ray realised he hadn't formulated a plan to hide or disguise his need for help. But looking into the general direction in question, the man nodded his head.

Returning some five minutes later he had with him a brown paper bag and pouring a small amount of its contents into his palm, he went on to explain,

"You make this like tea, but no milk or sugar; one cup in the morning and same before bed."

Nodding his head, Ray accepted the package, once the handheld sample had been carefully returned, not unlike diamonds into a velvet pouch.

"Will it work?" Ray wanted some assurances. After all, no actual mention of the exact problem was ever stipulated. Was it a cure-all? Would everyone who entered receive similar in the hope that the placebo would miraculously take action?

"Please," the man looked a little hurt, "do as I instruct and all will be well."

Then reaching for his wallet, Ray conceded, 'ah well, what have I to lose?'

"£20 sir and if you do not have complete satisfaction, please return and I will increase the potency."

Ray wasn't sure if he'd been had or not, but handed over the note in return for what he hoped wasn't just spiced up PG tips!

"All will be well sir, but please don't live your life like a reflection. The true soul lies within the person this side of the mirror."

Ray wasn't quite sure what was meant by the man's proverb-like advice, but he had plenty of time to ponder and decipher it, if he so wished. Then nodding his head in acceptance of the deal, Ray turned to leave. But before he could do so, the door swung open and a booming voice with an American accent filled the room.

"Hey honey, come on in, it's kinda quaint."

The words from the new customer had the effect of momentarily returning him to the real world, before the shop owner offered Ray a few last words,

"Bye now Sunny, take care!"

Ray froze as he re-entered the crisp brightness of the cold winter's day, however it was not the temperature that chilled him this time. Only one person had ever called him by the name of 'Sunny' before, but that was forty years ago and more importantly, only a short distance from where he now stood. It took him a few seconds before it dawned on him.

"He was referring to the sunny weather," Ray muttered to himself. "He actually said bright and sunny, didn't he?"

He would pass up on his initial decision to take the midday train home. Instead he would take the bus to the holiday camp he went to as a child and later as a young man. But hadn't it closed down? He was sure he'd heard it had, or maybe seen on a local news program, however even a derelict site would still bring back fond memories.

It was not to be though; in its place stood a brand new retirement complex, some still under construction; even the lay of the land looked unfamiliar. It was hard to imagine the joy, laughter, heartbreak, in fact the whole compass of emotions that surrounded decades of summer holidaying families that once resided here. Making his way along the beach also brought back no familiarity. A huge structure believed to be a nuclear power station had been selectively erased from his memory bank. 'Surely it was always there?' but he just could not recall its existence. The only remnants that now remained were a concrete ramp that once led to the seafront from the camp and an old stone tower that he imagined gave name to the resort that once stood there.

So it was to be here that Ray closed his eyes in vain effort to re-live his memories. But unlike some movie storyline, the vision of those joyous days would not return. 'Ah well, time for home, you can dream can't you?' Maybe he might see it again under different circumstances, but exactly how escaped him.

The next day Ray woke with an erection; not just any erection but the likes of which he had not experienced since he was a young man and what's more, it would not go away, even after he had dealt with it. The reluctance to normalise took over an hour.

He wanted to shout out 'Melissa, come back and give me my money's worth!' but he knew there would be no second chances. She had dispersed with his money like a 'fart in the wind.' But had it really worked? Or was it some kind of mind over matter or the power of belief in the magic potion, only time would tell.

The handwritten note pushed through Ray's letterbox left him smarting. He was hurt, not upset-hurt, or saddened, it was ego-hurt. Pammy it seemed had dumped him.

"She's dumped me?" Ray was aghast, it was incredible that someone who should be grateful for a man such as he, could actually put an end to their relationship. Maybe that description of their liaisons was a bit strong; probably the better use of terminology would be 'turning up when it suits.'

But she's gone, the words 'Please don't call again, I feel used and I'm off to my sister's in Newcastle' were the gist of the short, but poignant letter.

"Well I won't be jumping on the train to come and find you, you fucking..." Ray stopped himself finishing his bitter sentence. "She's probably right, I am selfish, but that's me, I can't change the way I am can I?"

Now it seems just as the latest problem was solved, that door of opportunity was firmly closed. Or to put it another way, his rejuvenated manhood is all dressed up and with nowhere to go.

**Chapter 50** **Present Day**

It was 9pm by the time Ray walked through the doors of the White Lion. For many years it had been Rays 'first port of call' but since Cyril's retirement, the early doors crowd, along with their banter had one by one dropped away. The present landlord was too young for the job and in Ray's opinion, couldn't hack it.

"What will it be Ray?"

"A pint of bitter please," as if Ray should have to be asked! Sat on Ray's stool at the end of the bar was Danny, nothing but a lad he appeared to be, carrying the troubles of the world on his shoulders.

"What's the matter Dan boy? You look like you've lost a shilling and found a sixpence." Ray tried to lighten the youngster's mood.

"What?" Danny's mind was elsewhere.

"It's an old saying when someone looks like you do, ah never mind." This wasn't the time to be explaining bygone phrases to the youth of today.

"Oh sorry Ray," and climbing down from his lofty position, Danny realised he was sat in Ray's place.

"No no, you sit there, its ok." It was time to relinquish the seat anyway.

"So, why the long face?" Ray asked, resisting his horse joke.

"It's nowt."

"Come on, nothing's worth blubbing into a good pint for." Ray tried to cajole him into opening up.

"It's my girlfriend, she's cheated on me." Danny looked truly upset.

"So have you chucked her?"

"Yeh, well I did, but she wants to make another go of it. I just don't know what to do. You're a man of the world Ray, what would you do?"

"You might be asking the wrong man son, but could you live with it?" I mean, will it eat away at you or can you let it go?" Ray tried to be diplomatic, even though he knew what he would do.

"I just don't know, I like her a lot, no, I love her. That's what makes it so hard."

"Is she sorry for what happened?"

"Oh yes, she says it was a stupid, one-off mistake." Danny's eyes searched Rays for a solution.

"Well why don't you have her back, but take it one day at a time?" The advice leaving Ray's lips went totally against the grain, but it was time for some compassion.

"Do you think it would work?" Danny looked hopeful.

"What have you got to lose? Tell her the ground rules up front, if it works it works, if not, at least you know the score." Ray was quite pleased with his profound words.

"Did you ever get it all wrong Ray?" He looked up to Ray for a crumb of comfort and would find some solace in the knowledge he was not alone with life's struggles.

"Oh yes son, oh yes. I got it wrong many, many times," but he wasn't ready to catalogue them all to the lad.

"You concentrate on your own dilemma, I'm going to put my feet up over there," and nodding across to a comfy chair in the corner, Ray left the ponderous Danny to his thoughts.

Taking his seat Ray chuckled to himself,

'Have I ever got it wrong, oh yes, and been stitched up too, not everything was my own fault.' He remembered the likes of Reg Priestley and his scam to get hold of Ray's pay-off from Jim at the farm; and more recently, his television episode. When his interview was screened it was squeezed down to a snippet, sandwiched between the ramblings of Ronnie and Marjorie. They had both been plied with alcohol and were incoherent. Firstly, his long pause, before he composed himself, was aired, making him look lost and gormless. Then after more drivel from Ronnie, his only verbal contribution was, 'Cheap booze at the supermarkets and immigrants.'

Not until the program hit the screens did he realise who was behind the set up. It was Ian Faraday, brother of Lorraine, his posh conquest as a young man. As a small boy, Ian had followed the pair and witnessed his big sister embark on her life's sexual journey. To him it was pure evil, he was sick to the stomach and swore that day he would get even. Turning up at the television studios a week after the screening, Ray finally learned of the man's bitterness straight from the horse's mouth; and what of the women in his life, not exactly a success there? Val and Beverley, the mothers of his sons, brought back no fond memories at all, although Angela was one exception. Then barring one other, his many encounters with the opposite sex were easily forgettable. But Ray was tired, more than ever, he was oh so tired.

The music made Ray feel good, it was an upbeat number from the late sixties that he couldn't quite remember the name of. His whereabouts too, the place was familiar but the exact location where he first heard it was a mystery. Then slowly it came back to him, he was at the Pontins holiday camp. A smiling Dawn was returning from a solo boogie. 'Come on, the music is slowing down. You too...' someone else was being asked to join them. Looking around, Ray could see it was her son. The three of them embraced as they moved in time to the sedate tune being played. 'I love you mum, I love you too Ray.' The boy with no hint of disability spoke so softly that it faded into the music.

"Time to go Ray," the tired landlord gave him a nudge to wake him from his unintended slumber.

"Quiet isn't it?" Ray searched the room, but Danny had left; probably just as well, he had thought of a pun to rib the lad. But by saying 'did somebody have it in for you?' regarding his girlfriend's infidelity, would have been a shade cruel.

"Yeh, not really worth opening on Mondays and Tuesdays anymore," he wearily replied.

As the door closed behind him, the bolt slid heavily across into its housing. The cold rain in the damp November air stung his eyes, leaving him chilled. Pulling his collar up in a vain effort to repel the night's clutches he then reached for his cigarettes. Opening the packet, 'last one' he reflected and covering it with his hand he lit up, drawing long and hard on its content. Taking a soulful look at his old friend between his nicotine-stained fingers, he quickly sheltered it after a large droplet of rain soaked into the white paper at the mid-point of its length.

No pedestrians or motorists bothered to venture out on this foul night; he just had the tired yellow flickering streetlights for companions. Then taking his first step onwards, Ray had in his mind that this was no ordinary journey home.

From high above, the ground could be seen rushing towards the new force with its pre-determined appointment with fate. Ray knew too and by the time his knees had buckled, he had already descended into darkness.

Bouncing off the pavement, the heavy raindrop met Ray's tear falling from his crestfallen eye with perfect timing,. Together their union created a new energy, a new entity, a new life. Just in the way his life had been mapped out from its conception to this exact point in time where the two unrelated waterous forces met. So after all, the life of Ray Taylor couldn't have ever been any different, could it?

**Epilogue**

All in all, seventeen people turned up for Ray's funeral. Amongst the mourners, much speculation was of his diary released by the police when no suspicious circumstances surrounding his death were discovered. Its pages contained little or no entries, except for erratic circling with several asterisks on the date of his death. One possible answer was that he had self-prophesised the date of his own end. But the more down-to-earth pointed to the fact that it was also his birthday, so the jury remained out.

As his casket was lowered into the ground, a ray of sunshine briefly showed its face through the heavy rain clouds. Maybe it was his thanks for remembering his frequent comment, 'not the crematorium, I hate the crematorium.'

A few short words were spoken at his graveside by recently-retired, straight-talking MP and charity fund-raiser, Sir Steven Blockley, who uncharacteristically yet openly could not hide his tears at the loss of his old friend.